I0636462

3797 Countdown

By Jude McGregor

Copyright

3797 Countdown, First Edition

Copyright © 2012 Jude McGregor

All rights reserved. No part of this publication can be reproduced, stored in a retrieval system, or transmitted in any form or by any means, electronic, mechanical, photocopying, recording or otherwise, without the prior written permission of the publisher.

While every precaution has been taken in the preparation of this book, the author(s) and publisher assume no responsibilities for errors or omissions, or for damages resulting from the use of information contained herein. All persons, events and images depicted herein are purely fictional; even if based upon real persons, events and images.

Nostradamus citations taken from *Nostradamus and His Prophecies*, by Edgar Leoni, 1982 edition, Bell Publishing Company.

Biblical citations taken largely from *The Holy Bible According to the Latin Vulgate*, 1874, Thomas Kelly Publisher.

Additional biblical citations taken from *The New American Bible*, 1987, World Bible Publishers, Inc.

ISBN 978-0-9853635-1-2

http://www.3797countdown.com

Published by 4D Productions

http://www.4dproductions.com

Made In The USA.

Contents

Forward

Before anyone gets any further in this book, let me set some things straight right off of the bat. I did not set out to write this book. This is not some lifelong pursuit of mine; it is merely something I had to do. I am not looking to make a lot of money or get famous or any other accusation that might surface upon its release. The book quite simply wrote itself and I was simply the tool by which it was written.

Why did I write this book the way that I did? That is hard to say. I wrestled with the 'how' of writing the book more than the 'what' I was writing about. Such is the nature of these things. I considered making it a scholarly book; however, trying to present these ideas and concepts in a purely scientific or scholarly manner would make the book too difficult for most people to read. Not to mention that much of it is the stuff of pure speculation and with little else besides argument, inspiration and interpretation to support some of the ideas, the effort to make their presentation 'scientific' would be futile.

I have, therefore, chosen to write this down in a style I call 'conversational literature.' In other words, I am presenting some ideas, theories and concepts through a conversation being conducted in the story. There will be places where the book seems more 'heady' or intellectual than others and, in contrast, there will be times when the book will seem more vulgar than it needs to be. In those respects, I am trying both to show the seriousness of the subjects and create a sense of 'realness' with the fictional characters in the story.

The theme of this book is what I call 'eschatological speculation.' It is a series of what I believe to be possible truths about the end of the world wrapped up in a completely fictional story being told about fictional characters. I am writing it because I do believe that some of the interpretations and ideas that will be presented throughout the story may just hold true, no matter how much I might wish they do not. In the end, however, this book is just a story being told; having completely fictional interplays between the characters and at times it may be shocking in ways unexpected.

There are certain ideas and concepts that are universal in nature. By that, I mean, they are found repeatedly throughout the universe, as we know it. Whether we (as a people, society, culture, etc.) believe in these things is not really the issue. I will say this before you start reading the story: "Just because you do not believe in something does not make it un-true." Likewise, I will also say: "Just because you do not believe in something does not mean it won't affect you."

JM

Introduction

Charles Geiger Jensen, born June 6, 1966; died September 11, 2010; buried September 13, 2010. His funeral was a couple of months ago. Standing there amongst our high school friends, his grieving mother and the rest of the mournful attendees, I could not help from seeing the bitter irony of his untimely death as I held his ex-girlfriend's hand. She was my fiancée by the day of the funeral and is my wife now. She'll be the mother of my first child in June.

Charlie was hit by a truck while running across the street in the morning the day he died. The driver of the truck was not charged, as the police believed his version of the story that Charlie had run right out in front of him. There were no other witnesses to refute his story, anyway. His truck had a 9/11 bumper sticker on it and the driver's name was George Oliver Dudley.

As we stood in the rain listening to the preacher's sermons and prayers at the funeral, I could not help but hear Charlie's words ringing in my ears, "One of these days, because of what I've done, I'm going to be struck down by God himself." The coincidence of the initials of the name of the man driving the truck was not lost on me, although some could argue that it was 'just coincidence'. If my time with Charlie taught me anything, it's that there is no such thing as 'just coincidence'.

I was staying with Charlie at the time of the accident, and I knew he always was careful around streets and intersections, as he truly believed that he would meet his end being hit by a vehicle. He was right. I was staying with him because he was explaining some things to me that he had figured out...things that people aren't supposed to know...things that may have carried with them a curse. He told me all of these things and made me promise to write it all down if something ever happened to him.

Well, something did happen to him...so here it is.

In the beginning...

Charlie was a friend of mine. I wouldn't say we were best friends but we were pretty close. I take that back. Now that I think about it, his name is the only one that ever comes to mind when someone asks about "best friends" so I guess he was. Anyway, we grew up and went to school together as part of a pack of friends who were all supposed to keep in touch after graduation. Of course, that never quite works out except for the ones who stay close to home.

For people like me, who travel a lot and move away from the old home town, it's tougher to stay caught up with everyone as the years drag by. Still, even as a traveling consultant, I would try to get back down to Tampa, FL at least once or twice a year to try to keep in touch with the old crew.

These visits usually involved getting as many of the group together as we could and meeting at our old haunts, eating pizza and drinking beer and sharing 'war stories' from our lives since the last get together. Plus, there was the requisite amount of reminiscing about the 'good old days' too. Everything stayed fairly light and casual, with the conversations never getting any more serious than 'who was dating who' or 'who divorced who'.

Whenever I did get to town and could make one of these get together's, Charlie and I would usually end up splitting off from the main crowd and talking privately about more serious topics. We just seemed to 'get' each other more than the blathering goofballs we claimed as 'friends' in the rest of the group. Oh, sure, we liked our high school buddies just fine but it always seemed to the both of us that the rest were always too caught up in the day-to-day world and didn't spend enough time noticing the real world around them...the bigger picture.

One of Charlie's main hobbies, if you could call it that, was comparative religious studies; wherein he had spent years of his life researching the various world religions and associated mythologies and cultures. We used to talk for hours on end about the things he found out in comparing the Aztecs and the Greeks, or the pre-Christian influences on Christian rites and rituals or some other tidbit he had found. I was always fascinated by his stories and found them much more interesting than the local gossip being spread by the others in our bunch.

Of course, our little party group, like the rest of the nation, was devastated after the tragedies of September 11, 2001. The whole country was in shock for months as our military struggled to lash out at as many enemies as they could to fight back against the invisible foe that had attacked us that day. Everyone who was an American spent the next few years internalizing the shock, the visuals, the grief and the horror of that day in their own way. Some may still be in shock or still recovering.

Our group did no better than the rest of the country in the aftermath. There was a stretch of about three years I didn't even visit Tampa; I did not 'want' to be around friends…and I couldn't imagine wanting to get together and laugh about the old days with them for a very long time. Given the lack of phone calls I received during that time, my guess is that the feeling was mutual among all of us.

After a few years went by, though, I finally got a phone call from Kelly, one of the girls from our high school bunch. I should say "women" instead of "girls" as we are all quite grown up now but it's funny, in my mind everyone in this group will always be "boys and girls" because I always think about them in terms of when we first knew each other. I guess that is part of the attraction of getting together so much, in that we all remind each other of our younger, sexier, more vibrant selves.

Anyway, she got in touch with me and told me the gang was going to meet again and it was far enough in advance that I could manage my consulting schedule around the date and even managed to set up a business meeting during the stay, so the trip was a write-off for me anyway. I figured, even if getting the old crew back together ended up feeling 'funky'; I could use the trip to try to drum up some new work and still come out ahead. Plus, the thought of seeing Kelly again was enough to get me excited about the trip. She sounded beautiful on the phone and I wondered if she still looked as good as I remembered from the last time we got together. She ran a beauty salon, so I figured she probably still did.

In the meantime, websites like Facebook, Twitter, MySpace and LinkedIn and other networking sites had become very popular and I was getting back in touch not just with the usual crowd but other people from my past that knew me from school or other parts of my past. I mention that only because sites like that let you find out more about each other's current lives than the informal, once-a-year get together's that end up being more like Bruce Springsteen's *Glory Days* song than hearing actual new news.

So I made the trip, had my business meeting and found myself later at the same local haunt we had always met at on Thursday nights. I was the first person there, as my meeting ended earlier than the time most of the others got off from work. As I sipped my beer and lazily scanned the sports news on the bar's TV, I wondered how this would feel, us all getting back together after the three-year break and trying to act as if nothing had happened. Or would everyone be dwelling on it still?

One by one, the old gang started drifting in. There was David, the onetime football star turned Chiropractor; and Randy, the onetime Thespian turned real estate agent; and Melissa, the onetime Cheerleader turned Admin Assistant for a crappy CPA; and, of course, Craig, the crappy CPA that Melissa worked for; and a few others too insignificant to name here. There was no sign of Charlie, however. I hadn't thought of calling him ahead of the trip, I had assumed he'd be at the bar with the rest of us.

A few hours went by as I waited for my friend to show up. I played the game of smiling and laughing at tired stories and stale jokes. Whenever someone would start talking about 9/11 or the terrorists, I would just drift off to another pairing and find a lighter conversation. Twice I pulled out my cell phone and dialed Charlie's numbers. The number I had for his home phone was disconnected, so the annoying pre-recorded message told me. His cell number was still recording voice messages, so I left a couple...asking him if he was coming out or not. I didn't get a call back, which made me curious.

I grabbed my fresh cold one that the pretty blonde behind the bar had just set down and went back to mingle, this time with a purpose. I approached several of the smaller, paired-off groups from the bunch and asked about Charlie, if anyone knew where he was or if he was coming. Most of them hadn't heard from him in years. In the more 'popular kid' crowd, I got a few glares from David and Randy; and Craig just told me, "Don't even get me started."

I asked back, "What the hell does that mean?" but the whole group of them just moved away from me like I had insulted their mothers or something. I took my half-empty beer and moved to a tall table near the outskirts of the group and closer to the door. My tab was paid up, so once I was finished with the bottle in hand, I was going to leave for the comfort of a different bar filled with total strangers.

I scanned the crowd of once-familiar faces a final time as I lifted my beer, confident I could guzzle the remainder and be done with this whole surreal, *Twin Peaks* like experience. It was as if any minute now the crazy backwards talking dwarf from that show was going to start dancing around in front of me. I drained the bottle and slammed it down, hard enough to make my statement but not loud enough to disturb my strange friends. That's when Kelly walked in.

Damn, she was still smoking hot. None of that 'having babies fat' or plastic surgeries crap…she was just as beautiful as she was back in school. But she now carried herself with a much more confident, sexy swagger than she did back then. Yes, I'll admit it…I'd always had a crush on her and had never done anything about it in all these years. She was a girlfriend of Charlie's back in school and, from what I heard on the grapevine, they had kept an on-again, off-again relationship ever since. In fact, I think it was a couple of 'incidents' with her that caused both of Charlie's divorces.

She quickly saw me, as I was sitting closest to the door, and rushed to my table. She was all warm hugs and what seemed to me a bit overly excited to see me. "How are you doing honey? I haven't seen you in years," and she hugged me again, pressing our chests together noticeably.

"I'm doing all right I suppose. Have you heard from Charlie? I asked around and got some strange responses," I quizzed her.

She looked over at the main group on the other side of the room and waved them off. "They are all idiots and assholes. Charlie is ok, he's just been getting into some weird shit lately and he spooked a couple of them," she told me.

"What's up with his phones? I tried calling…"

She put her hand up, interrupting me. "He moved, changed numbers…basically went into hiding after he upset the 'boys club' over there." She jerked her thumb towards Randy, Craig and David. "Want to get another beer, I'm thirsty," she told me.

"Not here, let's go down the road a bit," I replied.

"Fine with me sugar," she winked as she got up to leave with me. "You driving or am I following?" she asked.

"You drive, my car is safe here," I answered back with a smile. She smiled back at me and we headed towards her Mustang.

"Good old Kelly," I thought to myself, "still smoking hot and driving a Mustang. It's good to see some things do stay the same."

We got in without much small talk. "Where do you want to go?" she asked.

"How about Jesse's Tavern? No one from our group ever goes there," I answered back.

She smiled and nodded knowingly back at me. We drove the short distance and she squealed the tires into their lot, slamming the brakes just before tagging the rear end of a car backing out. "Ahh, there's a spot," she quipped as she slammed the car in reverse to give the other driver room to back out. "Nice coincidence," she said with another wink. As soon as the other car was clear, she sped into the spot and stopped the car. "We're here!" she announced proudly.

Kelly was not a girl who wasted much time, so I had to scramble to keep up with her as she jumped out of the car and headed towards the door to the restaurant. I caught up with her in time to get the door, to which she flashed me another smile and said, "Oh, a gentleman I see."

"Anything for a beautiful friend," was my daring reply, my heart pounding from the anxiety of throwing the compliment out there.

She ran her hand across my cheek as she slid by me, making sure to rub up against me more than necessary considering the size of the doorway. Or was that just my imagination? "Silly high school fantasies," I thought to myself as I eyed her swaying hips walk to the bar area. I followed quickly behind her, not wanting to get lost in the shuffle as she pressed past the others in her way, on her quest for our drinks. The crowd was pretty busy but all were complete strangers to the both of us; and the crowd made for a nice excuse to stay close enough to her to smell her perfume.

"What's your poison?" she turned and asked me with smiling eyes.

"Vodka martini, extra dry," I called back, adding, "You know, James Bond style."

She called out to the bartender, "Let me have two Ketel One martinis, extra dry, and bruised with 2 olives each."

She looked back at me for a sign of approval. "Perfect," I told her with a grin. "Damn, this girl sure knows her martinis," I thought to myself.

When she got the drinks, she handed one to me and clinked her glass against mine and took a sip. I took one too and asked, "What are we toasting?"

"Just seeing you again," she twinkled as she smiled, "let's find a place to talk."

She led the way through the bar crowd to a small table under the TV in the corner across from the doors. The location was perfect, as I had no interest in what was on TV and we could easily see who was coming and going from the restaurant before they could get in earshot. She paused at her chair for a moment looking at me and smiling. Shaking myself out of my stupor, I quickly reached over to pull her chair out for her to sit down.

"Good man!" she thanked me and giggled at the game she was playing. I couldn't help but let a small laugh escape as well, knowing she was having a bit of fun at my expense. It didn't matter with Kelly, at least not to me…and I think she knew that all these years.

We both took a healthy pull from our drinks and set them down. She sat waiting expectantly but not offering anything without a question being asked, so I did.

"So, what the hell's going on with Charlie?" I finally blurted out. "And why are Randy and Craig and those guys giving me strange looks and acting like they did?"

"Okay, darling," she started, then took another drink of her martini, "here's how it is." She looked me directly in the eyes and continued, "Charlie is in a very strange place right now, mentally speaking. I see him every now and then to make sure he's still ok but he could use a friend like you on his side." She went on, "I'll have to let him tell you the details but basically, he was really hit hard by the whole 9/11 thing."

"Weren't we all," I interrupted, taking a healthy swig of my drink.

"Yeah, well you know Charlie always was into the ancient cultures and religions and crap," she explained, "He really went a little crazy with it after 9/11 and then his Dad died a year later. That didn't help things any. Besides the grief, his Dad left him enough money that he could hide away and work on his research even more than ever."

I looked at her while I listened to her talk about our friend. Clearly by the ways her eyes welled up, she was still in love with him...always had been. I could hardly believe what I was hearing, though, as Charlie was always such a socialite within our group; but then again, he was as obsessive-compulsive as they come when he got inspired about something.

Kelly pulled an olive off of the pick with her full, red lips and chewed on it thoughtfully. "You know, now that I think about it, you probably are the only friend he has who could even understand what he's been talking about lately. Do you really want to see him?" she asked, almost as a challenge.

"Definitely," I confirmed as she pulled her cell phone from her purse. I started eating the olives from my martini as I heard her talk to Charlie.

"Hey sweetie, are you still up?" she asked him with a giggle.

"Well, you know...sometimes you go right to sleep after I leave," she responded to whatever he had said to her. She looked over at me with a naughty grin and a wink as she listened to his response to that.

"Hey, I'm sitting here with John and he wants to see you. Do you want to come out or do you want us to swing by?" she asked him. Clearly he hesitated because after several moments, she added, "Well?"

He must have given in because a few moments after that she told him, "Good, we'll finish up our drinks here and head on over."

She shut her phone down and put it back on her purse, then picked up her glass and raised it again. "To Charlie," she announced.

"To Charlie," I replied and clinked her glass with mine and we downed our drinks, setting our empty glasses down on the table at the same time.

"Hmm," she muttered as she looked at me differently than I was used to all of our lives. She appeared to be thinking about something to do with me but I had no idea what. So, I asked her.

"What?"

"Oh, nothing," she giggled a bit nervously, "just something Charlie and I have been talking about. Let's go to his place." With that, she got up to leave. Knowing how fast she gets moving once her mind is made up, I quickly got up to follow her out the door to her car. We jumped inside and I got buckled up as she laughed at how quickly I strapped myself in.

"Do I go a little too fast for you, sweetie?" she quipped.

"I'm just making sure I don't fall off the ride," I quipped back; and she seemed to enjoy the more playful banter we had going more so than in previous meetings and gave me a very sly grin back as she slammed her Mustang into gear and backed out of the parking spot. She chirped the tires twice getting out onto the main road and headed to Charlie's place.

The Genesis of an idea...

Kelly whipped her Mustang into the apartment complex she was looking for, a decent little place off of Waters Avenue near Dale Mabry Highway. I noticed as we pulled in that within walking distance was a bar, a 7-11, a gas station, a Cuban restaurant, a package store and a tanning and massage spa. "Good old Charlie," I thought, "always keeping his options close to home."

I could barely keep up with Kelly's driving as she zig-zagged through the complex's parking lot, finally pulling into an empty space after several turns.

"We're here!" she announced excitedly and immediately popped her seat belt off and was out the door. I scrambled to follow and caught up to her on the sidewalk headed to building number four. She started fumbling for her keys as we stopped in front of apartment number "444".

"I wonder how he managed that," I thought to myself, "Charlie always did have a fascination with numbers, especially the prime numbers that made up the number 12. Looks like the perfect address for him."

Suddenly, the door pulled open and Charlie was standing there in the light of his foyer. He must have heard Kelly jangling her keys or something.

"Charlie!" Kelly exclaimed as she jumped to hug him warmly. He hugged her back but was looking past her at me.

"Hey, bro," he said simply, "how's it going?"

Kelly pulled back off of him and let Charlie and I meet. I walked up to shake his hand and said, "hey yourself and I should be asking you that question!'"

He held my hand firmly and brought his other up to my shoulder, saying, "It's really good to see you, John. Come on inside, you'll have to excuse the mess."

I followed him and Kelly inside and saw an apartment that looked something like Fox Mulder's basement office from the *X-Files* TV show. There were books everywhere, all with yellow stickies sticking out of them, marking the pages for whatever reason. The walls had maps of the world taped to them, alongside flip chart sized pieces of paper with partially legible numbers and phrases on them. There was even an *X-Files* "Trust No One" poster hanging on the wall in the back corner of the living room to complete the scene.

As Charlie moved some piles of books around to clear some places to sit on the futon and armchairs, Kelly moved around his apartment like she lived there. She went into the kitchen and asked us both, "We were having martinis earlier, do you guys want me to make some more?"

"Yes!" Both Charlie and I answered at the same time. Kelly giggled at the two of us and set about mixing up a homemade batch for the three of us.

"So, you like martinis too?" he asked me, "vodka or gin?"

"Vodka, of course," I answered him, adding, "you know…007's."

"Oh, right, of course…the James Bond thing. Well, good because that's how Kelly makes them," he said and looked at her in the kitchen with real affection on his face. He turned back to me and said, "and since she likes them that way, so do I," and he winked to get his point across.

That was always the thing with me and Charlie…we 'got' each other's meanings with very few words being spoken. One mention of my youthful fascination with the James Bond novels and he knew exactly how I liked my martinis, no need for further questions. Just as I knew, by the timing of his wink, that he knew that I knew about Kelly and his relationship, nothing more needed to be said.

But he was stalling and I knew it, so I pushed him, asking, "So what's the deal with you and the crew from high school?"

He grimaced at the question and started to explain, "How do I put this…I figured some things out and tried to share it with some people and it didn't go well."

"Okay, what does that mean?" I kept prying.

"Well, I had Randy and Craig over and was trying to show them some of the things I was working on and it got into a big argument and Craig hit me," he informed me.

"Those guys are just assholes!" Kelly added as she came in to the room with our drinks.

"Now sweetie, don't go getting all worked up again," he tried to calm Kelly and sat her down next to him on the futon. I took a seat in the empty armchair next to them. We all took a deep drink from our glasses and I was impressed with Kelly's martini making skills. She had my favorite martini down to a science. "I'll have to remember that," I thought secretly.

I took a second drink and continued, "So you moved here and aren't talking to the old bunch anymore?"

"That's about it. You know how clique-y they can be," he pointed out. Again, he didn't need to say much more. Our crowd had cliques even within itself and clearly Randy and Craig had already started spreading the 'word' about Charlie to the others. It explained the reactions I'd received from the group at the bar earlier very easily.

That being said, we all three sort of paused on our own reflections for a few moments, sipping our drinks and eating the olives while we thought. I had this feeling like when you are about to jump off of a high dive or bungee jump, like I was about to 'take a leap' or something. I scanned around the room at the big pieces of flip chart paper on the walls and the many piles of books lying around.

"So, what's this crap all about? What got Craig so upset?" I finally asked, unsure if I really wanted to know the answer. You never knew with Charlie.

"The fact that he has a pea brain!" Kelly blurted out and tipped her glass up and drained it in a final gulp.

"Hey baby, why don't you mix us up a fresh batch," Charlie pointed to her empty glass with his own and added, "and this time, make them a little dirty."

"A little dirty, hmm?" she taunted him back, putting her hand on his thigh and licking her lips with her tiny pink tongue. I was turned on just watching her; I couldn't imagine how he kept his cool that close to her.

"Yes, honey, just a little," and he leaned over and kissed her cheek, moving her hand away at the same time.

"All right, all right, I know…I'm interrupting," she said as she picked up our glasses and stepped over piles of papers and books to get back to the kitchen.

Charlie leaned in towards me as if to emphasize his next point, "Dude, do you really want to know? It's not light subject matter and it's going to take more than one night of martinis to explain it all."

"Sure, why not?" I replied almost carelessly. How bad could it be anyway?

"Seriously, how much time do you have down here?" he pressed me for an answer.

"I made my reservations for just the weekend but I could stay longer I suppose," I told him, starting to really think about it. I was between projects after all and the last one had been a cash cow, so I had some money in the bank and some cash in the market that was available too.

While I was thinking this, Charlie added, "and you can stay here too. Seriously, I can make some room and you can crash in the spare bedroom. It has a pullout sofa-bed and there's plenty of bars and restaurants and even takeout around here."

"Hmm," I thought to myself and muttered out loud. Charlie sat back and let me consider his offer. He could always tell by the look on my face when I was seriously crunching something in my mind and gave me the time to think. If I wasn't spending money on the hotel room and eating out every night, I could spend some serious time in the old hometown hanging out with Charlie and Kelly. "Hmm," I thought again.

"Are you sure I wouldn't be a third wheel?" I asked him, glancing over at Kelly shaking the martinis up in the kitchen.

"Nah, she'd be ok with it," he assured me, adding, "that's something else we need to talk about but when we are alone."

"Are y'all talking about me?" Kelly called from the kitchen as if to announce she was coming back to the living room.

She handed me my drink and I playfully told her, "You bet…but it's all good!" with a wink.

She smiled at me really big and then turned to set hers and Charlie's drinks down on the coffee table in front of the futon. With her back to me I looked at Charlie to gauge his reaction to my flirtation and he winked and made the "A-Okay" sign with his fingers, quickly lowering them as she moved to sit down next to him.

"Okay," I thought to myself, "I am getting curious about this other conversation about Kelly now." I sipped the fresh martini, noting the tinge of olive juice flavor that was added. I looked over at Kelly approvingly, saying, "Hey, dirty is good…who knew?" and smiled.

She patted Charlie's thigh, then squeezed it and taunted me back, "dirty is always good in my book." She raised her glass and I followed with Charlie joining in. Without actually touching glasses, we toasted, although I had no idea what they were toasting…I was just drinking it all in, both literally and figuratively.

After we drank and sat our glasses down, Charlie asked me, "Well?"

"Well, what?" Kelly turned to ask him.

"John here was going to tell me if he really, really wants to know what I'm working on and how long he has to hear what I have to say," he told her, putting me on the spot in front of her.

I picked up my glass and took another healthy sip as they both waited for my answer. Again, that feeling of jumping off a cliff shot through me but, then again, with Charlie out of the 'crew' there weren't many friends I had left. Besides, he had always treated me well and, except for him and Kelly, there really was no other reason for me to even visit this town any more. "Screw it," I thought to myself as I put my glass down and finally looked them in the eyes.

"I can say a month, maybe two," I stated matter-of-factly.

"That's great!" Kelly blurted out.

"Yes, it is," Charlie added, "but what about the other part? Do you really want to know? It's pretty heavy stuff."

Now, if any one of our friends told me that Charlie was getting into 'pretty heavy stuff' I'd have waved them off. I knew Charlie liked very serious topics and mysteries and was not easily intimidated like the rest of the high school crowd was; but with Charlie telling me that…knowing our history together…that did make me a little nervous.

"Okay, before I commit to anything give me some idea of which ballpark we are talking about please," I asked him back.

With that, Kelly pulled away from him and Charlie sat up and looked straight at me, "Armageddon."

"You mean like in the Bible Armageddon?" I retorted.

"Yep," he continued, "I figured some of it out. Not all of it but I think I have enough of the book of Revelations and other prophecies figured out that I think I know where we are in the story and what's going to happen next. Still interested?"

With that he picked up his drink and fished an olive out and started chewing on it as I thought.

"Okay," I internalized my inner arguments, "that is serious stuff; but it's Charlie and he does usually do his homework before he starts talking about things. Again, how bad could it be?"

I repeated that last question out loud to Charlie, "How bad is it?"

Charlie paused as Kelly excused herself to the bathroom and she went into Charlie's master bedroom. He paused and waited for her to leave the room.

"It's seriously bad, Dude, I'm not going to kid you," he confessed. "You've seen how our friends reacted to you and there was one girl, you didn't know her, she listened long enough that when that hole in the Gulf started spewing oil, she killed herself. That's the part Kelly doesn't like to hear. There's actually a curse on some of what I've done."

"A curse?" I asked nearly disbelieving, "really? Like with the mummies in Egypt?"

"Worse," he replied, "it's in the Bible. I can show it to you if you like."

"No, hold on…let me think about this," I told him and really started thinking about it.

Kelly came back in to the living room and told us, "I'll make you boys one more batch of martinis, and then I'm going to bed."

"Thanks babe, you're the best," Charlie told her as she leaned down to get his glass and kissed him on the forehead. She whispered to him, "good luck." I don't think I was supposed to hear that but it made me understand just how much this meant to them both.

She came to me and took my glass as I just finished draining the last of my drink and winked at me and sauntered off to the kitchen one last time…for the night anyway. The sway of her hips as she walked away was not lost on me; and I think Charlie caught me looking at least once that night.

I sat thinking hard. "This is something I can do…but is it something I want to do?" I pondered. Again, I considered that, except for Kelly and Charlie, there was little else bringing me back to Tampa. Without those two, the rest of the group was not going to be enough for me to 'care' enough to visit any more. I also considered our relative ages and when, if ever, I'd have another opportunity like the one being presented to me now. And I considered how I'd feel being under a supposed 'curse' if I did stay to hear his story. As I weighed the pros and cons, Charlie sat patiently, watching my face for any signs he could pick up on.

Finally, after quite a bit of thought and more than a little worrying, I looked up and told him in all seriousness, "Dude, I'm down for whatever you've got to tell me. I can spend at least a month with you and, screw it, I'll listen to what you've got…no worries…I can take it."

Charlie could tell that I had thought very hard about it but still had his doubts. He asked again, "Are you sure? Curse and all? I mean, if this ruins your life or changes your outlook, it will be my fault."

He picked up his pack of cigarettes and lit one up as he waited for my answer. I watched as the dancing flames of his lighter lit the burning end of the tobacco stick in his mouth. I had just quit smoking a few months earlier and, to be honest, I'd not had a real 'craving' until that moment; a moment I somehow knew would change my life completely.

As if sympathetic to my situation, he turned his head up and away from me, blowing out the smoke from his lungs purposefully in another direction. He then added, "No pressure but dude, if we do this, we have to do it for real…no shrinking out on me."

I saw the seriousness in his face as I continued to run through the possible scenarios and outcomes in my mind. Kelly came back and returned our glasses, now full again with a fresh batch of 'dirty 007's'. This time she said nothing but set our glasses down and kissed both Charlie and I on our foreheads as she did so. I looked at Charlie again to see his reaction but he simply watched her and his eyes followed her out of the room as she went to his bedroom to get some rest.

As soon as she was out of the room, his eyes returned to me and he looked at me expectantly, waiting for my answer. I thought about it a bit more before realizing just how bad Charlie needed someone to talk to that wasn't going to fight him; and how badly Kelly wanted Charlie to have a human connection he could relate to. Strangely, as with people driving slowly past a car wreck so they can see the damage, I couldn't deny the morbid curiosity that was developing in my brain after hearing the small bit of info I'd heard so far.

I reached for my glass and he did the same. I needed a drink to give him my answer; and he needed one to hear it.

"Screw it, I'm in," I told him as the vodka stung my lips and tongue.

"Are you sure?' he asked me again as he drank from his glass. To be fair, he was giving me every opportunity to back out with no shame…and I respected him for that. Because of that and the many things he had done for me…with me…over the years helped to steel my resolve.

"Yeah, I'm sure," I reassured him, "I'll stay as long as it takes and listen to everything you've got."

"Excellent!" He smiled a big smile and raised his glass to me. I raised mine back; little knowing what I had just signed up for but certain that it would be an interesting ride, no matter what happened. "We'll get started tomorrow after we get you out of that hotel."

With that, he got up and went to the closet in the hall where he pulled out a pillow and some sheets.

"These should work for tonight, we'll get you moved in properly tomorrow," he told me as he set the handful down on the coffee table, on top of a stack of papers.

"No worries," I assured him as I continued to sip my martini and think about the decision I just made. "How bad could it be?" kept echoing in my mind as I looked around at the books, papers, flip chart pages and other crap lying around his apartment. There sure was a lot of it, which meant he had done his research and there were going to be a lot of explanations to come to cover it all.

As I sat sipping my drink and pondering my fate, Charlie drained his glass and set it down on the coffee table. "Time for bed for me," he announced, "you stay up as long as you want or crash. It's fine with me either way. Make yourself at home." He walked over to my chair and patted my shoulder and said, "You have no idea how important this is to me, John. I'm glad you are here."

"No problem Charlie," I assured him even with the doubts flying around my brain, "happy to be here."

With that, he squeezed my shoulder a bit then walked off to his room. He didn't shut the door completely and I could hear him wake Kelly slightly as he crawled into bed with her in the next room. I sat alone in the eerie darkness of his poorly lit apartment, surrounded by books and papers unfamiliar to me at the time, and sipped my drink watching the shadows dance in the corners of the darkness.

"What have I gotten myself into?" I thought over and over as I drank that last martini and sat alone in Charlie's living room listening to the soft sounds of a couple having late night sex and trying to be quiet about it. I looked around at the papers and books, resisting the urge to get up and look closely at any of them. I was sure that each, in its own time, would be explained to me over the coming weeks. I thought about the equally strange but optimistically playful banter between me and Kelly earlier and what conversation the two of them had about me that they kept referring to.

After I drained the glass, confident there was enough liquor in me to get to sleep even in those surreal surroundings, I picked up all of our glasses and moved them to the kitchen quietly. I went back to the futon and threw the pillow down and laid the sheets out as best I could at 1:00 am with a good buzz going and lay down on them. As my eyes quickly got heavier and harder to keep open, I could hear the quiet mumbles and soft giggles of my two best friends in the next room but had no idea of the mental train wreck that was headed my way…courtesy of the two of them…or the strangely morose and simultaneously jubilant outcomes of my decision to stay.

Exodus from reality…

The next morning was busy. Kelly had to get up early to go home and change before going to work and I found out that she's not a very quiet morning-person. She got in the kitchen rattling around glasses and dishes and tidying up for Charlie. It was a harsh wakeup that early in the morning with the previous night's drinks still in my system. I groaned at the headache I had, somehow knowing it wouldn't be the last one I'd have during my stay. I curled over under the covers and tried to ignore Kelly's noisemaking, hoping that the sofa bed in the other room might be easier to deal with in the mornings she stayed over.

Then she completely surprised me. The clattering in the kitchen stopped and I couldn't hear her for a moment or two. Then I felt her hair on my exposed cheek and the warm perfume of her breath on my ear.

"Have fun with Charlie today sleepy head. I hope he doesn't scare you off because I am looking forward to your being around too. Oh, and please remember that he takes this stuff very seriously, so even if you don't believe it, try to at least understand it."

Then she kissed my cheek! I was paralyzed with surprise and excitement and was broken from the spell only when she closed the door to Charlie's apartment as she left moments later. I could still feel the warm press of her lips on my skin and knew she probably left lipstick on me. "Better wipe that up before Charlie sees it," I thought and drifted back to sleep, smiling.

I was awoken about an hour later when Charlie punched me in the arm lightly and laughingly asked, "Making time with my girl I see."

I quickly shot up and my hand moved to my face to wipe off Kelly's lipstick from earlier, trying to mumble that nothing had happened when he started laughing even harder and waved off my explanation.

"Do not worry about it, dude. It's not a problem, I was just messing with you," he said. "You need to get up so we can get your car and stuff from the hotel."

He was right; there was no time to waste with Charlie, especially if he's on to something that he's passionate about. So, I jumped up from the futon and gathered my clothes from last night and straightened up as best I could. I found some mouthwash in the guest bathroom and used it to clear the taste of olives out of my mouth. I tussled my hair a bit then decided I looked about as good as I was going to get. So, I went back to the living room where Charlie was waiting/

"You ready?" he asked.

"As ready as I'll ever be," I retorted. I was not a morning-person.

He got up to leave and put on a pair of sunglasses and handed a pair to me, "Take these…you're going to need them."

"Nah, I'm fine as is." I answered dumbly, not knowing what was coming next.

"Fine with me," he said and we approached the front door and he opened it. I was not prepared for the huge blast of sunshine that burned into my brain as the door swung open.

I shielded my eyes with my arm and muttered, "Oh shit!"

"Told you," he said, handing me the glasses again. This time I took them.

"Yeah, my apartment faces due East, so mornings are a little bright," he explained as my eyes adjusted to the glasses and the glare. We walked out with Charlie leading since I did not know what kind of car he drove. Turns out it he drove a sweet Lexus sports coupe.

"Nice car," I told him.

"It's a pretty sweet ride," he answered back, adding simply, "Dad's money."

"Ahh," was all I said to that. Thanks to Kelly, I knew the rest of the story about his father dying and leaving him some money. I got in the passenger seat and we left to go get my car. We drove most of the way to the parking lot my car was at in silence. We were both slightly hung over, both wearing sunglasses and both feeling like we were just running errands to get to the really important work at hand.

So, we got to it. We went to the bar where my car was in silence, listening to classic rock on his radio. Springsteen was singing about the "Glory Days." It was eerily appropriate and more than a little coincidental, considering I'd been thinking of that song the night before in the same bar we were driving to. We soon got there and Charlie pulled into the parking lot and drove up to my car. He said, "I haven't been back to this place since Randy and Craig came over."

I let that comment go without adding to it and unbuckled my seat belt to get out. "Hey, nice ride yourself, dude! Where did you get that?" he asked me.

I looked over at the black and chrome Cadillac STS that was my 'nice ride' as he put it. It was, way more car than I could normally afford and it got crappy gas mileage but it was fun to drive. It was fully-loaded with the premium luxury sports package and boasted a 350 horsepower Northstar engine and a tricked-out sports transmission. It looked like a jazzy 'old person car' but drove like a four-door Corvette. I liked it a lot.

"I had a really good project with IBM for a couple of years that just ended. It was a cash-cow project, so I was able to bank some decent money," I explained, adding, "it was either that or a Harley and I decided the Caddy looked more professional."

"And a whole lot safer!" he responded, tapping my arm with his fist as he joked. "I'll follow you to the hotel," he added.

I got out of his car and double checked my pockets: wallet, ok…keys, ok…hotel room key, ok. I opened my car's door and got in and fired her up. I loved the way the engine would rev up to speed when she started, like firing up an Indy car or something. She even tells me "Hello, John" on the dashboard display when I get in. She's a very friendly car, in my opinion.

I backed out of the parking spot and turned to leave the lot, watching for Charlie in my rear view to make sure he followed. He did. With the street pretty clear of traffic, I bolted out of the lot to show off my car's speed a bit for my friend. Not too fast but enough to get a jump on him and make an impression. I watched in my rear view as Charlie zipped out after me and quickly caught up. I smiled as I thought about the ageless saying about 'boys and their toys'. We got to the hotel in no time and parked side-by-side.

"Does this place have a bar?" Charlie asked, getting out if his Lexus.

"Yep, right over there," I told him, pointing my finger at the sign that read "Oasis Lounge."

"I'm going to see if I can get a beer while you clean up and get packed," he told me as he walked off.

I looked at my watch; it read 10:00 am. "Good luck," I called out to him. He simply raised his hand and waved back.

I went to my room and got busy packing my stuff. I took a quick shower, shaved and fixed my hair then put on some clean, comfortable clothes. Once I was dressed, I scrambled to unplug everything from my laptop, pack up my mobile office and clothes and stuff; and get back to work with Charlie. A couple of trips out to the car to load my luggage in the trunk and I was ready to leave. After checking out at the front desk, I went to find Charlie. Sure enough, he was sitting at the hotel bar with a half-empty beer, swapping stories with the bartender.

"You ready?" he asked, seeing me come in the door.

"Yep," I answered simply, ready to get on with it.

Charlie slapped a $100 bill on the bar and told the bartender to "keep the rest" and got up to leave with me.

"I can't believe they were open," I half-asked him as we walked out together, amazed he was able to get a drink this early and surprised at how generous he was.

"They weren't but the bartender was here early and it's amazing what a hundred dollars will buy you in this economy," he offered for an explanation.

We walked out of the hotel towards our respective cars, and I observed the peculiar visual metaphor that our vehicles represented. They were black and white, 2-door and 4-door, Japanese and American...both fast and sleek but different in subtle ways, just like Charlie and me.

"I'll follow you this time," I told him as we were getting in to our cars.

"Try to keep up," he replied with a wink.

"No problem," I smiled as my mind answered him mentally. We fired up our engines and sped out of the hotel's parking lot to get back to his apartment. He, or rather 'we', had a lot of work to do.

Things were all business as soon as we got there. Charlie told me to unpack my car while he cleaned up the guest room. That was the room he kept his main computer in, but it also had an un-used dresser and sofa-bed; and more importantly, a door to close to keep Kelly's early morning noisemaking at bay. As he moved piles of books and papers out, I moved my suitcases and laptop in.

"Go ahead and use the dresser, I think most of the drawers are empty," he suggested to me. "Put your laptop wherever you want and make yourself at home. After all, if I don't make you run screaming out of here, you'll be living here for awhile."

I unpacked quickly and set my computer up on the small end table beside the sofa-bed. I called my house-sitter, Mary, who was watching my condo and taking care of my dog for me while I was out of town. I needed to clear with her that she was ok with my extended visit. She was, very much so actually. I was relieved that she was available to watch the place and my pet for me; and she needed the work, so she was normally happy to hear when I needed to be away for long periods of time.

"Did you get a big contract?" she asked, curious as to why I wasn't coming home as scheduled.

"No, just staying with some old friends," I told her; and asked her to fill out a mail forwarding card for the post office and gave her instructions on sending me a few things that I would need while I was at Charlie's. Once that was done, I started my laptop up and got online to update my statuses on Facebook, LinkedIn and Twitter.

"Staying in Tampa town longer than expected," was all I wrote, ensuring plenty of questioning comments as a result. I chuckled to myself as I knew the vagueness of the status would probably bring a number of "why" and "what's up" comments and other questions from my personal and professional connections. I didn't even have time to close the website screens when I saw that Charlie 'liked' my Facebook status from his iPhone. It was a little strange to see that, because Charlie so rarely got on Facebook anymore that I'd nearly forgotten he was in my friends list…but knowing that he liked my status confirmed without asking him that he was glad I was there.

I looked around the small room to take it in one last time as a 'normal' person…that 'falling off a cliff' feeling starting to rise again. I took a deep breath and sighed, then went to the living room where I knew Charlie was waiting expectantly. It was about Noon.

As I stepped back into his living room with the books, and papers and flip chart pages, I saw Charlie sitting on the futon putting the finishing touches on a joint he'd just rolled.

"Still smoking that stuff, huh?" I asked as I came in.

"Hell yeah," he responded verdantly, "I'd go freaking crazy without it. Besides, with everyone else except you and Kelly being ignorant idiots, the stuff I've been working is pretty nerve-wracking."

"So you've told me," I shot back taking a seat in the armchair next to him where I had sat the night before.

"I'm really glad you stayed, man," he spoke in between puffs while lighting up the doobie. "It sucks not having anyone to talk about this stuff with." With that he took another puff then held the hit in to get the rush of calm it seemed to give him. He handed it to me and asked as he eventually exhaled, "You want some? You might need it."

I thought for a second as the thick blue smoke from the end of the joint wafted up towards me, then took it from him. "Just like old times, right?" I joked as I took a deep hit in. It had been years since I'd smoked any weed. I'd nearly forgotten how harsh the smoke was and how heady the high could be until the smoke I took in started hitting my lungs and brain.

"Whoa," I muttered through the smoke and passed it back to him. The head rush was almost immediate and the familiar feeling of the high that came with it started taking over.

He took another deep pull from the joint and passed it back. "Keep it," he told me as I took it from him. He exhaled his hit and continued, "Just sit and listen…hear me out."

I nodded and continued getting high as he was gearing up to speak.

"Okay, here it is in a nutshell: it is very possible that the world is going to meet its end in 3797 AD. We are in the time period most commonly referred to as 'Armageddon' and no, it's not the end of the world, it's just the third of the four 'torments of man' and the beginning of the whole process." He held up his fingers to make quote marks in the air to indicate when he was quoting things. He continued, "What happened on 9/11 was so 'biblical' in its proportions that a lot of crap started flying around the Internet about it but most of it was just crap; so I went back to my books and started looking for clues in the various prophecies and predictions; and well, I kind of figured out the connection between the Revelation story and Nostradamus' book."

"Whoa!" I thought to myself, still puffing on the diminishing doobie as he spoke. He reached over for it, indicating that he wanted a hit and that it was ok for me to talk. I passed it over to him and carefully thought about what he just told me.

"Nostradamus…wasn't he like two years off or something?" I asked. I'd seen something about a prediction of his involving 1999 or something like that.

Charlie's eyes lit up and he finished his puff and passed the roach back to me to finish.

"I am so glad you said that, that is a great place to start the conversation!" he exclaimed, then jumped up to find a book. After looking in a couple of places, he found what he was looking for: a copy of *Nostradamus and his Prophesies* by Edgar Leoni. "This," he stated very seriously as he held up the tome for me to see, "is THE definitive book on the subject of Michel de Nostredame." He emphasized the word 'the' and made a point of pronouncing the name in his best French accent. He continued, "Never buy anything else on the subject…the people who talk about 'green languages' and channeling his spirit are all full of crap."

"Just who is he?" I asked curiously.

Charlie explained, "Nostradamus was, and still is, a much disputed man who lived in France during the Middle Ages from 1503 to 1566. He was a self-styled astrologer and mathematician and said to have been incredibly intelligent. He was also a doctor; however, the majority of his great work with the plague victims in France was done before he actually finished his degree. By his own claims, using the arcane methods of the forbidden 'black magic' and quite possibly accompanied by ingestion of some of his own self-made prescriptions including heroin, he would sit with candle and bell in a dark room and have his visions. He would 'see' things happening in different places around the world and in different times. He also claims that his visions were the result of divine intervention, a gift from God, since not everyone who tried his methods could see as he did. The notes that he wrote about the things he saw in his visions evolved into quatrains, each quatrain being a four-line verse. He organized these quatrains into groups called 'Centuries' that contained 100 quatrains each, except for Century VII which oddly was not finished or only contains 42 on purpose. There are many other disputed predictions and works out there that claim to be written by Nostradamus, however, some of these are so badly faked they resemble the Internet emails circulating around today."

He went on, "Now, to make sure that you understand, I will explain a few things. First of all, the most famous of Nostradamus' works is a book called *The Milliade*, or 'The Millennia' in English. It is made up of hundreds of predictions and these predictions are the quatrains; and are the predictions by Nostradamus that the majority of people, both the supporters and detractors, write about. They are by far the most popular part of Nostradamus' works that people argue over. The book, however, also contains a Preface and an Epistle that are largely ignored by the 'pop' supporters and debunkers. In addition, the book itself was designed by Nostradamus to be part of the puzzle too. The fact that it's called "The Millennia" and is made up of 'Centuries' instead of chapters all has meaning."

He flipped hurriedly through the pages looking for the right one. "There!" he excitedly declared, "read this one" and put the book down on the coffee table and pointed with his finger.

Quatrain number X-72 reads, in English:

> "The year 1999, seventh month,
> From the sky will come a great King of Terror;
> To bring back to life the great King of the Mongols,
> Before and after Mars to reign by good luck."

"Let me explain how this works, at least in my case," he went on, "I believe that when you are trying to figure out a prediction, particularly one by Nostradamus, there are certain guidelines you have to follow, or you simply become one of the hundreds of supporters and detractors who argue nonsense back and forth. First of all, if you are looking at a quatrain, you have to consider the entire quatrain. You cannot just take a line or two or three from it and try to explain it. You have to acknowledge all four of the lines for each individual quatrain. Secondly, you have to understand that each line has its own meanings, as well as the quatrain as a whole when all four lines are put together. Lastly, you must stick to the limits of translation of the original work. You cannot just arbitrarily change words or lines in his predictions so that they better fit what you think they are talking about. You either make the argument work correctly or you move on to the next one."

"Okay," I replied simply, a bit overwhelmed by the rush of the pot and the information he was giving me. I was trying to absorb it as fast as he talked but it was difficult.

"Now, everyone else out there says 'he was two years off' but he wasn't. Let me ask you a question: when did the War on Terror start?" he asked expectantly.

"Right after 9/11 when Bush called it out," I replied, fairly knowledgeable of those events myself.

"Wrong!" he exclaimed. He rushed over to a stack of printed out news articles from the far corner of the room. He shuffled through them as he walked back. He pulled a few of them out of the stack and handed them to me. I read through them as he continued.

"So, for line 1, the 'sept mois' could mean 'seventh month,' which most try to say that means 'July 1999'. The Roman calendar at Nostradamus's time started in our March, however, making 'Sept' or

'September' seven months into our year. Also, the literal use of the term 'sept' implies the word-play he is famous for and adds a double-meaning for this, indicating September over July; rather than his using "septieme" which would be "seventh" more properly stated in his language and is the word he uses in nearly every other quatrain where that number appears, marking this particular prediction at September 1999."

He went on, telling me, "For lines 2 and 3, we have a 'great King of Terror' who 'visits,' possibly traveling by plane, which is easy enough to imagine, to rouse up the great 'King of Mongols'. Now, what you have in your hands are news articles from September 1999, actually starting on Aug. 31st, where there were seven...yes, that's an important number to remember...seven successful bombings out of eight attempts, another very important number to remember, in Russia. The bombings were staged by Islamic terrorist groups from Chechnya who have ties with Osama bin Laden, who may very well have traveled to Chechnya, which was once part of the Soviet empire, to instruct or inspire the terrorists. That part we may never know for certain but can assume was possible. Mongolia, at its height during the reign of Genghis Khan, extended into both modern day China and Russia, so it could mean either country but there's a part of the Armageddon story in Revelations that makes me think he meant Russia or the Soviet Union."

I stared at him dumfounded as he read through his notes and continued, "Moscow was hit very hard, hundreds were injured in different buildings and many were killed. The Russian Vice President at the time, who would be President by May of the next year was Vladmir Putin. He is nearly mentioned by name in another prediction and he declared a 'War on Terrorism' which went largely ignored by the rest of the world at the time, especially after the 9/11 attacks. To support Putin's position and Nostradamus' description of his rise to power as the potential 'King of Mongols, nearly two years later on August 17, 2001, just 2 weeks exactly prior to 9/11 and when Putin was the President, there were news reports coming out that the actual Genghis Khan burial site might have been discovered."

"So, for line 4 I believe the 'Mars to reign by good luck' means 'war was narrowly averted'; rather than the actual movement of the planet, however, it could mean both and probably does; using the astrological and figurative meanings of that phrase at the same time would be classic Nostradamus word play. Mars had indeed just finished a doubly long stay in one sign and moved to another, ending its long journey on Sept. 9, 1999…which, yes, would be 9/9/99. Also, at the same time, according to Russian military officials, meetings occurred to determine Russia's reaction to the attacks, of which a calculated nuclear retaliation was discussed as a serious, viable option! Fortunately, in keeping with my interpretation of the prediction, Russia did not immediately respond, instead waiting until after 9/11 to join America's War on Terror." With that, Charlie sat back down on the futon, as if to wait for me.

"Holy shit!" my brain screamed in my head. I was amazed and chilled with fear at the same time. I could understand his arguments and, in reading the news articles about the Russian attacks I could see he that he could be right about them. My mind was swirling with his statements as I gazed at the simple passage, trying to grasp the deeper meanings of the words Charlie was telling me. I read and re-read the four lines and yes, he certainly did seem to have a logical translation figured out with this. The ramifications that it implied threatened my entire belief system.

"Need a minute?" he asked me, knowingly.

"Umm, yeah," I shot back sarcastically, reading the passage and the news stories over and over.

Charlie pulled out his special tray and started rolling another joint, speaking as he did so.

"As Sherlock Holmes is noted for saying in the stories written by Sir Arthur Conan Doyle, 'When you have eliminated all that is impossible, then whatever remains, however improbable, must be the truth.' He also warned against 'twisting the facts to fit the theory, rather than the theory to the facts.' The point being, that although we could sit and argue every particular point of each individual line and quatrain of Nostradamus to come up with any number of fantastic explanations, if the goal is to actually figure him out then we must use deductive reasoning and logic to decipher his code. Once all of the facts have been laid out and the possibilities examined, the impossible ones must be eliminated. The possibilities that seek to create or introduce un-verifiable variables must also be eliminated. What is left, however improbable, must be the truth...period."

The doorbell rang as I pondered that last statement.

"That's the pizza," he said as he put away the tray and he rose to answer the door. While he paid for the pizza and put it in the kitchen, I was lost in thought over his Sherlock Holmes comment. He did that on purpose because he knew I was a big fan of those books when I was younger, just like the James Bond stories and some others. The point hit home to me, he could be right. I wondered at how far he'd gotten with his theory.

He came back with two plates with pizza slices on them and set them down. "Do you want a beer, water, coke or something?"

"Yes, a beer would be great," I answered him, "it might help."

"Trust me, it will," was his simple reply.

He came back and handed me a cold one, which I happily accepted. I took a long sip of the beer, hoping to numb the growing ache in my head. We ate our pizza in silence, although I have to admit I wasn't feeling all that hungry. I knew I needed to eat something, so I munched down as much of it as I could then took another drink.

"So, how does this relate to the Bible?" I asked, some part of me wanting to know more, to 'see the train wreck' so to speak.

I waited as he crammed the rest of his piece of pizza in his mouth and chewed on it. I think he was chewing slowly on purpose to plan the next part of the conversation out. When he finished chewing, he challenged my patience further by taking a long pull from his beer.

"Before we do that, let me tell you that just because I can match these things up that you don't have to go running to church, per se'," he instructed. "Nostradamus and the Christians aren't the only ones who have these types of prophecies about the 'end of times', there are many others, including but not limited to the Mayans, Aztecs, Egyptians, Hindus, Hebrews and many others. In fact, besides Nostradamus, the Aztecs also identified 1999 as the beginning of the end of times. So, like I said, it doesn't mean you should start building pyramids or changing religions either."

"Okay, I see what you mean," I said as I thought, "so since there are so many pieces to the puzzle it doesn't mean anyone's 'right' in the end."

"Exactly!" he jumped up off of the futon and agreed. "I mean if that was the case I'd have gone Aztec and started ripping people's hearts out...ha, ha!" He joked but I knew with Charlie, sometimes there were hidden meanings behind his laughter.

More Revelations...

"Come over here and read this part of the story," he signaled me to follow him, so I got up and did so. Along the wall behind the futon was a large, wooden pedestal upon which sat a huge, leather-covered Bible with a brass lock and corner braces. The cover alone must have been over an inch thick and the book was very old. Charlie carefully opened the brass lock and pulled the majority of pages aside. I noticed he did not have any sticky notes in this book, as he searched through the pages.

"Catholic now?" I asked curiously, as Charlie had always been pretty agnostic about things.

"The Bible is, of course, and the older the better!" he shot back, "they invented the Christian religion so, if you're going to research Christian beliefs, they are the original source. Look at the *Da Vinci Code* and *Angels & Demons*, that author seems to agree with me. The Catholics at the same time have the keys to their religion and a few others locked away in that basement of theirs."

He found the page he was looking for and stepped back so I could approach the antique tome.

"Start at Revelation 13 and read the whole thing," he told me. As I read, the continued to speak keeping in time with me. "Okay, now you have to remember a couple of things as you read this that the difference between Nostradamus and Revelations is that the church is assigning a moral meaning to the events, disasters if you like, that are occurring in the story. Nostradamus is simply predicting the dates and assigning clues as to who-is-who in the Bible prophecies. The first beast that is being described here in the Bible is the 'King of the Mongols' in the Nostradamus prediction we just talked about, who I believe is the Soviet Union after they re-form and go back to their old ways."

"The reason I believe that is because of the reference to the '7 heads' and one of them being badly injured but then healed; and the reference to the bear. If the Soviets do re-form, particularly in response to Islamic terrorist attacks from Chechnya and the other countries in the Caspian Sea region, all the world would 'wonder' at them as they re-start their empire building under the reasoning of quelling religious uprisings in the re-conquered regions. I also believe that the 'beast' reference alternately identifies a main figure in the coming years and the 'beast of empire' that is or was the Soviet empire. That being said, the references to the number seven over and over again in this entire book are referring to what Nostradamus was trying to tell us with the title of his book, *The Milliade*."

"What do you mean?" I asked.

"Well, what a lot of people don't get is that Armageddon is not the 'end of times' for everyone. For the chosen, it is the painful birthing process that civilization is going to go through to get the world to the new 'Golden Age,' as the Mayans put it, or 1,000 or so years of relative peace without having to worry about world wars and evil empires and whatnot. You know, a lot of people think that a lot of the things in the Bible or in Nostradamus' book are things that happen instantly but they aren't. They are things that drag out over many years so that it only makes sense after it has long become history."

Charlie could barely contain himself as he continued, "A lot of other stuff is going to go on during the Armageddon time, which is about 25 years by the way, and the 771 or so years of earthly and cosmic calamities after the Golden Age. Crazy stuff like the Moon being knocked out of orbit and replaced by whatever hit it…or a chunk of it anyway. But that's what Nostradumus' main message was with the title of his book and calling the chapters 'Centuries,' because he is yelling at us every time we ask 'what does the seven mean? It means 'millennia'. The Soviets were the only nation that did empire building, particularly in the Middle East and South America, at the end of the 6th millennia, which ended on December 31st, 2000 for modern man's purposes, and is currently, as an 'evil empire' are nearly 'fatally wounded'; but if they do come back, this will all be true."

"Now flip to Century two, quatrain number 80 of the Nostradamus book," he said.

I walked back over to the coffee table quickly and picked the book up and found the page. I read the quatrain.

Quatrain number II-80 reads, in English:

"After the conflict by the eloquence of the wounded one,
For a short time a soft rest is contrived:
The great ones are not to be allowed deliverance at all;
They are restored by the enemies at the proper time."

Again, he spoke as I read, "In line 1, 'After the conflict refers to the Cold War that ended when the Soviet Union went back to being Russia and after 9/11 Presidents Putin and Bush announced that the US and Russia would work together on the War on Terror. The reference to the wounded one once again refers to the greater beast in the Revelation story. Line 2 refers to the 'strange alliance' between America and Russia post 9/11 and shows that it is a 'contrived' alliance, combined with the first line which refers back to the 'eloquence of the wounded one' and would imply Vladimir Putin by the fact that it was under his Presidency that alliance occurred. Line 3 indicates that the 'great ones' not being allowed 'deliverance' indicates that neither the U.S nor Russia will survive the torments. The last line, of course, refers to the dual attacks on Moscow in 1999 and the 9/11 attacks on the US two years later and the fact that the Muslims are responsible for riling up the two superpowers."

"Okay, now come back over here," he told me. I set the book in my hands down and returned to the old Bible.

Charlie continued, "When you get to verse 11, that is talking about the other 'great one' from the Nostradamus prediction, making the United States potentially the 'lesser beast'. As in both predictions, if you boiled down the stuff about morality and blasphemy and whatnot, you basically have the same situation in both books. Two great political and military superpowers, which the US and USSR are, one of which will go on a conquering rampage again and the other rising up against it. Going back to the Islamic terrorists, they are the 'synagogue of Satan' who are being used to put both of our countries in a very proud, nationalistic mindset."

"What about the '666'?" I looked up, having finished reading the verse.

"That is a great question, one I haven't fully figured out yet," he answered honestly. "Since the Soviets haven't re-formed yet, we don't know. The footnotes at the bottom of the page from the Catholics say that they are the name of a man with the numerical equivalent of six-hundred and sixty-six. That would mean you would have to use numerology to figure out whose names would fit that description...and I do not know numerology, so it's a wait and see for me. Or it could be something else altogether, like the fact that in 2000, which was the end of the 6th millennia for our purposes, it was determined that there were 6 billion people living in the US and 6 trillion living throughout the world...or it could be my birthday...who knows?"

My mind was spinning as Charlie kept speaking, "And if you notice, not everyone has the 'number of the beast'. The prophesy says that they have to have the mark, or the name, or the number in order to do business, which is how the Soviets used to act, by trading only in their currency and only with other Communist countries. This new 'democracy thing' they are trying out is already wearing thin on their economy already and in fact, just a couple of years ago there were news stories talking about their own people wanting to go back to Communism. However, with them being the first 'beast' that means that this second 'beast' is going to try something similar. Remember the talks about National ID badges and even digital implants for US citizens?"

"Yes, I remember," I answered back weakly.

"That kind of crap right there will fulfill this prophesy," He explained, "never, and I mean NEVER get anything like that done. Move to another country, get out of here...that will be the mark."

I was dumbstruck as the similarity to what he was saying was merging with recent history and the present.

He went on, "The funny thing is, however, if you are a devout Catholic then you can't believe in numerology or astrology because the Church banned it years ago. So, only us outsiders can actually do the work of solving the puzzles in their own book. Now, before we go any further, let me show you another passage real quick," and he reached past me to turn the pages again. I stepped back to give him room and then he stepped back so I could return.

"Okay, the final Revelation, number twenty-two, just to warn you," he pointed down the page to the bottom.

I read the passages and then I looked up and over at him, "Wow, that's serious!"

"Yeah, I don't know if that curse applies to me or not but you know, sometimes I think that one of these days, because of what I've done, I'm going to be struck down by God himself," he told me. I got a noticeable chill and he continued, "But it's like I said the Aztecs and Mayans and other cultures have prophecies that align with the ones from St. John and even Daniel from the Old Testament, so what does that mean? Become Jewish or Mayan or Aztec or Catholic? If they all are 'right' about the same thing, then which belief system do you choose? Clearly the Bible story is only interested in saving the Christians and everyone else are, and I quote, 'dogs, and sorcerers, and whoremongers, and murderers, and idolaters, and whosoever loveth and maketh a lie.' End quote."

We looked at each other for a few moments and I thought hard about everything he told me. "How about another beer?" I asked him, mentally exhausted for the moment.

"Sure thing, sit back down and I'll get us a fresh round," he said on his way to the kitchen.

I sat down in the chair, my head reeling from the possibilities that were being presented. I picked up what was left of my beer and guzzled the rest down while Charlie got us new ones. I was hoping the alcohol would numb my brain a bit, admittedly.

He returned and set my beer down and returned to the futon. I took a deep sip from the new, ice cold brew to add to my growing buzz. Charlie drained his first beer and got up to put the empties in the trash, giving me more time to think. When he came back the second time, he sat down and lit up the joint he had rolled before the now forgotten pizza arrived. I gladly reached over to take it from him when he offered it, took an unhealthy pull on it and shot-gunned another drink of beer down behind it.

I asked as I passed the joint back to him, "So, if the Soviets and the Muslims are the 'beasts' what does that make us?"

"Dude, you better hit this some more and finish that beer," he advised me and we did just that in silence. All the while the pot and beer were having their desired effects on me, I kept wondering if this fantastic story of his was real or not. Combined with the stuff he was telling me, this whole trip went from being a little strange to downright surreal. We kept passing the doobie back and forth and hitting our beers until they were both spent. Now, quite buzzed, I got up and went to the kitchen myself to get another round of beer for both of us.

I came back in the room and set his down, asking, "So, are you going to tell me?"

"Okay…but you aren't going to like it," he replied. "You know how the Revelation story in general repeats a few times the 'alpha and omega'?"

"Sure, I've heard that or seen it a few times," I answered, curious where this was heading.

He reached over for a smaller New American Bible and tossed it over to me. "We don't need the big one for this. Check out Genesis real quick, I mean scan through it. Basically, you have God creating the universe, then the world, then plants, animals and humans. The snake and humans create sin, Cain kills Abel, Adam and Eve have another kid named Seth, you get a family tree breakdown of the connection from Adam to Noah and then he builds the ark, God destroys the world with water and afterwards, Noah and his kids pop out and get busy. In the meantime, there's that crazy crap about 'giants in the earth' and angels sleeping with earth women in Genesis 6 and the story where Noah gets drunk and he curses the son who sees him naked when he was passed out in his tent in Genesis 9."

"Yeah, I see all of that," I looked up and told him as I quickly scanned the pages to keep up with him.

"So, you've got a whole creation-destruction-repopulation thing going on right up front, explaining that 'as God giveth, so shall he taketh away' from us humans. That's the gist of Genesis 1-10. Now, turn to Genesis 11."

I did and started reading while he talked, "the very first story after the creation-destruction-repopulation between Adam and Noah is the Tower of Babel. It is like the world's first skyscraper and the key is that everyone in the world communicated with a single language, before God destroys it to 'confound' mankind. It is the reason that Babylon is called that, supposedly because that is where the original tower of Babel was built."

"Okay," I said, looking up again and waiting for his explanation.

He continued, "It is my belief that on September 11, 2001 our country in general, and specifically New York City, was marked as the 'new Babylon' by the World Trade Center towers coming down; and that, as new Babylon, the city of New York will eventually be turned to nuclear rubble. Edgar Cayce, another famous predictor of things who was an American, once was asked about Armageddon and he described that the city of New York would lie in ruins by the year 2100. This, of course makes the good ol' USA the damned drunken 'whore of Babylon'."

"Wait, so who is Edgar Cayce?" I interrupted him to ask.

"Edgar Cayce, much like Nostradamus, was a 'seer'," Charlie explained, "Although, unlike Nostradamus, Cayce was a reluctant prophet, so to speak. While Nostradamus set out to see the future in his *Milliade*, Cayce did not desire his particular 'gift' and did not make predictions of the future as a matter of habit. Normally, he would consent to making diagnosis of people's ailments, at their request, and prescribe solutions to make them healthy again. Many of these potions used combinations of heroin and rose petals or other parts of the flower, much like Nostradamus' own potions for curing the plague victims in France hundreds of years earlier."

He continued, "Cayce was born in the United States in the state of Kentucky in 1877 and lived into the early 1900's. By his own family's accounts, he was a simple country man who was frequently described as an 'unlettered rustic'. While awake, Edgar was just a simple man, from the southeast United States, with not much to say. When he went into a 'trance' however, he changed. He spoke clearly and succinctly and with a vocabulary his conscious self would not have understood. While under his self-induced trances, he would predict with amazing accuracy the nature of a person's ailments and the prescription for their recovery. On record, he has over 14,000 predictions and there's a society set up in Virginia just to study them."

"Whoa," I interjected, impressed at the numbers.

Charlie went on, "Again, unlike Nostradamus, Cayce did not seek to 'know' the future. He sought to help other people out; hence, most of his work is devoted to healing the sick. Although their individual motivations were different, the similarities and dualistic contrasts between Nostradamus and Cayce are un-ignorable. For one thing, they both healed people using their own peculiar prescriptions. In contrast, Nostradamus studied and worked very hard to achieve this talent and Cayce fell into it. For another, both men exhibited signs of being able to predict things at a young age. In contrast, Nostradamus pushed that talent to the limit, whereas Cayce almost gave it up on a number of occasions. In another aspect, Nostradamus was a student, learning by both formal education and his own 'midnight studies' of ancient religions, astronomy, medicine, mathematics, and a host of other occult pursuits. In contrast, Cayce was a 'country bumpkin' with little more than a below-average public education and rural country background."

"Perhaps the most important similarity," Charlie went on, "is that they both made startlingly specific predictions concerning the time the world is in now. In one such reading by Cayce," Charlie reached back to another pile of papers on a nearby table and found the sheet he was looking for quickly. He read the article to me.

> "As to the changes physical again: The earth will be broken up in the western portion of America. The greater portion of Japan must go into the sea. The upper portion of Europe will be changed as in the twinkling of an eye. Land will appear off the east coast of America.
>
> There will be the upheavals in the Arctic and in the Antarctic that will make for the eruption of volcanoes in the Torrid areas, and there will be shifting then of the poles - so that where there has been those of a frigid or the semi-tropical will become the more tropical, and moss and fern will grow. And these will begin in those periods in '58 to '98, when these will be proclaimed as the periods when His light will be seen again in the clouds."

"Seriously?" I asked in near disbelief.

"A lot of people think he was talking about 1958 to 1998, where we did indeed see a lot of problems with Tsunamis and earthquakes out west," Charlie offered, "but nothing as serious as Cayce is describing. No, I think he means 2058 to 2098."

With that, he set down his beer and got back up, saying, "Also, if I am right, the Revelation story of the end of the world is the Genesis story being played out in reverse, starting with the 'twin towers of Babel', the destruction of man to the point of extinction, the world being flooded and somebody building a ship, perhaps, and taking the chosen people and probably a bunch of other stuff off the planet with them. Want to know what happens to the new Babylon and potentially New York and our country if I'm right?"

I got up and followed him back to the old Catholic Bible. He flipped it over to Revelation 14 and told me, "read this and pay attention to the last six lines."

I read and he waited as I imagined over the many horrors the passages were describing. When I got to verse 14, Charlie started talking again.

"Okay, see the parts about the two angels with sharp sickles coming out of the clouds and 'reaping' the bodies of man, spewing blood and destruction for miles?" he asked.

"Yeah," I answered tentatively. I could already see where he was going with this.

"That's 9/11 dude," he stated gravely. He flipped a few pages in the book, "read chapter 17, verse number 18."

I looked down again and read the verses describing how Babylon would fall and the drunken slut that was supposedly our nation, ending with the verse that states that the woman represented a great city that ruled over the kings of the earth.

"Interesting," I said looking up, "why not Washington?"

"Washington is the base of American political power and it too was hit in the attacks but New York is the base of global financial power. The Twin Towers is where most of the nations in the world, at least 66 of them, all had offices and traded currencies, all based on the US dollar. Plus, New York is where the United Nations is located, a body that 'reigneth over the kings of the earth' as the Bible puts it. Most importantly for the symbolism of the story, it is also where the Statue of Liberty is located. Symbolically speaking, the woman is mentioned several times in Revelations, indicating the birth of our country, our relative un-involvement with the first 'torment of man' which was

Napoleon's empire march; and even our participation in the second torment that was Hitler and World War II. One passage even mentions her getting the 'wings of an eagle' and, of course, our main national symbols are the Statue of Liberty, a woman, and the American eagle. From what I can gather from reading the reasons for the punishments, the main problem, or sin, is pride. We as a country are too proud of ourselves, we don't celebrate the glory of God, we celebrate the accomplishments of men and women, athletes, and our military; but for all of our power and vast resources we fail to glorify He who gave them to us."

He continued, shaking his head as he did so, "Now we, as a nation, are 'drunk with power', we are removing God from government, money, schools, etc.; and are riding the back of our own enemies for the sake of our addiction to oil. I did the astrology for that day and we were under the sign of Gemini, or the Twins. The World Trade Center, being the 'twin towers of Babel' due to it being the second occurrence that signals the 'second coming', and everyone communicated to everyone else…country to country, and nation to nation…by computer translation and interaction, which means the whole world was communicating in Binary…machine code ultimately; which fulfills whatever the requirements are for the 'second happening of the Towers of Babel' from a 'the whole world was speaking the same language' perspective. If you consider both stories from that viewpoint, God does not want man to work together for man's sake; but only in unified worship of Him will we ever be truly one human family." Again, his fingers flew up every time he emphasized something in quote marks. "Besides," he added, "when Nostradamus refers to Washington or our government or military, he usually refers to us as 'the Romans' due to the overwhelming similarities between our empire and theirs, particularly the architecture in Washington."

I stood numbly looking at him with a mix of horror and disbelief on my face as he continued.

"Now look at Revelation 4," he told me and I flipped the pages.

"The first mentions of the four beasts are represented differently at the beginning of the story," he said as I read.

He continued as I stood stunned and read, "The alternate translation could be that Nostradumus was two years off, which could mean that

America is the 'beast of empire,' given the imagery of a flying eagle and we eventually 'nuke' the Middle East for our oil, rendering its lands completely useless for anything other than oil production for thousands of years, including the literal Babylon, which would be Iran and Iraq specifically, and all of the political crap they've put everyone through all these years. We've already killed Saddam and allegedly Bin Laden, so this cat-and-mouse game being played out could be the case; but I really believe my translation of that 1999 prediction is accurate and we haven't seen the last of the Soviets. I assume that the order of the beasts in Revelations 4 matches how they are presented later in Revelations 13. The third and fourth beasts from Revelations 4 are the ones from the story in 13; and, if we are one of the 'beasts' then they are reversed. From a US perspective, we would be the greater, first beast; which is the third beast in Revelations 4 and should be represented by a man, making the fourth beast in Revelations 4 the second beast in Revelations 13 which should be an eagle. I would argue that the US is represented by the eagle and that doesn't make sense because we aren't the 'lesser' of anything; and the numeric symbolism of '666' being the name of a man would better match the third beast from Revelations 4, given the imagery we have to work with."

He wouldn't stop and I was too dumbstruck to ask him to.

"However, we cannot help but notice that the visual image we are given for the fourth 'beast' is consistently an eagle. It shows up again in chapter 8, verse 13 during the trumpet blasts. Admittedly, right now, besides China, the United States is the closest thing to an 'evil empire' the Earth has; and if we are one of the beasts, the descriptions are vague enough that we could be either one. In fact, if you look at it from a time perspective, we could be the lesser beast in that our nation is indeed the youngest of all involved. However, you must remember that, although we can be one of the beasts and the whore at the same time...but we can't be both beasts. So, it's either the Soviets and Islam are the beasts and we're the whore; or America and Islam are the beasts and the whores together; or the Soviets and America are the beasts and the Middle East, along with everyone else, gets nuked along the way...and we're still the whore. I favor the third interpretation, as it appears to be the best explanation given what we have to go on."

"Another reason I favor my translation of the 1999 prediction is this: assuming that the pundits out there and Nostradamus are right about the first two 'beasts' from Revelations 4 being Napoleon and Hitler let's compare them. Both rose to power in Europe, both went on a conquering spree that stretched from Egypt to northern Europe, both involved the Jewish people in some significant way, and, most importantly, both butted heads with Russia. In both cases, the attempts to invade and conquer the Russians are seen by most historians as the turning points in their empire building wars. England got the credit for beating Napoleon and we took the credit for taking out both Hitler and the Japanese; but in both cases, it was Russia who caused their downfalls; as if the bigger 'beast' was repelling the attacks of the first two, lesser, 'beasts' back. I call it 'historical foreshadowing'. Interestingly, to this date, Russia has never really retaliated against the Germans or the French because of it; but that doesn't mean they won't eventually."

My mind swirled with images of world wars and mushroom clouds as I tried to keep up with Charlie's dissertation. I found myself nodding as he spoke, as I understood what he was saying, at the same time struggling to actually process the possibilities he was presenting to me.

He added, matter of factly, "Besides, there are always the Fatima visions to fall back on in favor of my interpretations."

I looked up and over at him as he paused. I didn't really know what he meant by 'Fatima visions' and must have conveyed that with the puzzled look on my face as I asked him, "What do you mean?"

"Well, there have been several apparitions of the Virgin Mary around the world over the last 2,000 years," he explained. "Each time she appears to a specific person or group of people and usually has a message of some sort, sometimes it's a broad-based prediction and other times it's a personal revelation for something specific. In fact, she reportedly appeared to a young native of Guadalupe, Mexico to have a church built in their area, for example."

"Okay," I responded, waiting for Charlie to get to the point.

"In Fatima, Portugal there were a series of these visions of Mary, primarily to three young shepherd girls between May 13th and October 13th in 1917. In these visions, she was appealing to the whole world to repent and obey God's will and, if the whole world did, then Heaven would grant the world peace. If they did not, however, she warned that

God would punish the world by way of wars, hunger and persecution of the Catholic Church, the Pope and all Catholics everywhere. Of course, as you and I and anyone else even vaguely aware of world events since 1917 can attest, the world did not repent and follow God's commandments. As a result, in contrast, several years later Hitler rose to power and the world was engulfed in World War II."

"True enough," I nodded my head in agreement, thinking of how opposite to 'following God's commandments' the world had gone since that time.

"The Vatican investigated the stories of the girls, and in fact a huge miracle was supposedly worked in the skies above Fatima that some 70,000 people witnessed on October 13th to give some credibility to the stories of the girls. The girls actually predicted the time, date and place it would happen and the witnesses all testified to the same story. After some time and in questioning the girls about the visions they had, the Vatican released some details about the message and meanings of the visions to the world. Besides visions of Hell and other details, there was a three-part prophesy given by the Virgin Mary to the girls to share with the world. Interestingly enough, one of the three parts has been kept a secret to this day; but the other two parts are fairly well-known."

Charlie paused for a moment and looked over at me. I was processing what he was telling me in light of what he'd already shown me in the Bible and in Nostradamus' book.

After a few moments to let it all sink in, I said, "And..."

"And here's the punch line," he leaned forward as he spoke and was emphasizing the words with the seriousness of the look on his face, "Mary told the girls that God had chosen Russia to be the means of punishing the world if we didn't obey. Basically, if everyone did repent and pray and follow God's law, Russia would be 'converted' and the world would be at peace; but if we didn't then God would use Russia to send the world into chaos. Which would make them a fit for them being the greater, first 'beast' in Revelations 13."

Charlie got up and walked over to a table with stacks of books on it. He quickly rummaged through them and returned with a small paperback. I could see the world 'Fatima' in bold letters on the cover. He quickly scanned through the pages he had sticky note labels on until he found what he was looking for. I braced myself for what was sure to be a stinging message.

He sat back down and resumed his explanation, "The essence of the message goes like this, the first part involved visions of Hell and Mary's plea for everyone to remain faithful and pray for the conversion of sinners and the saving of souls. In the second part of the secret, Mary specifically predicts the outbreak of World War II and emphasizes that praying for the conversion of Russia, to Christianity of course, is the essential condition for world peace. The third part of the secret has never been publicly revealed by the Vatican to the rest of the world. I think that piece of the puzzle is Russia taking the United States out of the picture, as we would be the only country that could reasonably be expected to stop them and, as I showed earlier, fits the interpretations of both the Bible and Nostradamus."

He paused for effect and glared at me with eyes nearly crazed from all that he had been studying. Then he read from the book in his hands, "According to the documentation we have, Mary said and I quote, 'If my requests are not granted, Russia will spread its errors throughout the world, raising up wars and persecutions against the Church. The good will be martyred, the Holy Father will suffer much and various nations will be annihilated.' Again, this all fits with my interpretation of the events of 1999, the Nostradamus prediction and how it ties in with the prophecies in the Bible, specifically with Russia, or the Soviets if you prefer, being the larger 'beast' and America being the lesser 'beast' represented by the eagle in Chapter 13 of Revelations."

I was like a deer stuck in the headlights of an oncoming car as he continued, "One thing I do know is that whoever the 'beasts' end up being, I truly believe that America is the 'whore of Babylon' and New York City, along with the rest of the country, is going to be punished with many disasters, both natural and man-made, in the coming years. We haven't seen anything yet. Oh, and the Muslims are the followers of the false prophet but more on that later."

I was dismayed and afraid and excited at the same time. Everything he was telling me made sense, in some sick, twisted, surreal way and I was not expecting what came next. I had been paying attention and following the story so far and it all seemed possible, as far as I could tell; but my mind was struggling to keep up with the plot twists and implications of what was being shared with me. What Charlie told me next blew me away more than the Bible stuff he was talking about.

"Oh, yeah," he started hesitantly, "Kelly loves you, by the way."

From out of the blue, he twisted the conversation from Armageddon to love…I nearly couldn't believe it. I marveled at how his mind could process so many different things at the same time; and at the same time sat in disbelief that we could be having these conversations at all.

"What the hell are you talking about now?" I asked, nearly frantic with fear and struggling to keep up with him.

"She more than likes you," he said quite matter of factly, "we've talked about it and, except for me, you are the only other guy she likes enough to actually consider being with. If something ever happens to me, I want you to take care of her…marry her even."

"Marry her?" I quipped, "she never wants to get married, she told me that much herself."

"She won't get married now because I won't marry her," he explained, "but if something ever does happen to me, she won't have that excuse anymore. Plus, if something does happen to me because of all of this, you'll know I'm wrong about the religion thing and she'll need someone to make an 'honest woman' out of her. Seriously, promise me you'll take care of her for me. We've talked and you are the only person she thinks about besides me in that way." He was nearly begging me at this point.

"Okay, I promise," I told him. Who wouldn't make that promise, particularly in my shoes? She was an un-requited love, a crush that was not satisfied for me; and it made a lot of what had happened previously between us make a lot more sense too. Not that I wanted anything to happen to my friend but he was right. As creepy as the work he was doing was, if he got 'struck down' it would scare the crap out of both Kelly and me; and we would be all that was left for each other of the old high school crowd.

Fornications...

The fact that he had mentioned Kelly in the middle of talking about the 'end of times' and the 'whore of Babylon' really bothered me. Surely that talk didn't include us, did it? I mean, if it did, then we were all part of the problem, right? Then I remembered Charlie's words about the Aztecs. I silently hoped he was right - just because a culture or religion had prophecies that rang true, didn't mean that we had to become followers of each and every one. Maybe these predictions were just events, events that religions had wrapped morality around to hit their point's home with.

Our conversation had died off. I was lost in thought, considering all that Charlie had told me that afternoon. I was at the same time terrified and excited. After all, finding out that the world was in Armageddon was one thing but knowing that Kelly wanted me sexually was quite another; and something that seemed much more real and tangible. The mixture of the thoughts in my head was disturbing to say the least.

Charlie had gotten up from the futon and went to the kitchen to clean up. No matter what you had against him, you had to admit he kept the place clean. Dirty dishes appeared to be his pet peeve, well one of them anyway. I watched with little interest as he moved about the apartment, cleaning and moving piles of paper around. My body was aware of my surroundings but my mind was miles away, thinking about all of the things we had talked about through the day.

I got up from the chair and walked over to the small opening between the living room and kitchen wall where I could see Charlie straightening things up. "I'm going to take a nap, my head hurts," I told him directly through the opening, nodding my head towards the guest bedroom instinctively.

He looked over at me and nodded in agreement, "Okay, man, take a break. I'll try to be quiet...I might take one myself. It's been a crazy day, right?" He added, "Kelly might wake you up, just saying."

"Whatever," I answered back disbelievingly. I didn't want to learn any more 'secrets' this day. What we had talked about already had my head spinning as it was. Trying to mix my desires about Kelly in with them seemed 'sinful' somehow, in a way that I'd never felt before. I walked off to the spare bedroom and lay down on the sofa. I didn't bother pulling the bed out; I just needed a soft place to land and a pillow for my throbbing head. I pulled out my iPhone and checked the news, my stocks and my Facebook account quickly…and found nothing noteworthy enough to capture my attention. I turned it to 'vibrate' and set it down behind me on the end table and drifted off into a lazy afternoon nap.

What seemed like hours later, I vaguely remember the sound of the door to the room opening and then closing again very quietly. Then the smell of Kelly's perfume hit my senses and further pulled me from my slumber. Then the warm feel of her breath as she whispered into my ear.

"Hey handsome, are you still asleep?" she asked with a taunt in her voice.

My eyes fluttered open and as my focus cleared, I saw her kneeling down to talk to me wearing a thin white bath robe. The view down to her cleavage was not lost on me, nor was my appreciation of it lost on her.

"See something you like?" she teased me.

"Why yes I do," I teased back, looking back up into her glittering green eyes.

She leaned over to kiss me, this time not on my cheek but pressed her soft, warm lips to mine and kissed me as a lover. I was lost in the kiss, reveling in the taste of her mouth, tasting her inquisitive tongue, and breathing in the breaths she was breathing out. We kissed for quite some time, I simply allowed myself to enjoy the moment until I felt her hand start moving down my stomach. I reached out with my own hand to grab her wrist and stop her from going further and pulled my head back away from her kiss.

"Okay, what's happening here, Kelly?" I asked her directly, moving to sit up as I did.

"I thought Charlie told you," she explained with a worried look, "I like you and I was just feeling a little frisky is all."

I looked at her, with her pouty face and glittering green eyes and those soft, warm lips. I couldn't tell what she did, or did not, have on under the robe.

"Does Charlie know you're here?" I quizzed her.

"Yes he does, in fact he swatted my butt after I put this robe on and told me to 'get in there'," she told me, still making the pouty face with her lips pursed. "Besides, it's not like Charlie's the only guy I go out with. He knows about the others, who mean nothing to me by the way. You, on the other hand mean a lot to me and I'm curious to be with you."

With that last line she came over to the sofa where I sat and stood directly in front of me, her torso a mere foot or two away from my face.

"Besides," she said, looking down at me and unraveling the belt around her waist, "are you saying you don't want a piece of this?" and she pulled the robe open and let it fall to the floor. She did a quick spin to show me everything. She was wearing only a pink bra and matching pink thong panties. She looked fantastic, she still had a knockout body and I was really seeing it for the first time in years, since we used to go to the beach together.

I looked up at her then stood up, placing my hands on the sides of her face, "of course I do, Kelly," I reassured her. "You are certain that Charlie's ok with this?"

She then brought her hands up to my face and said simply, "Yes," and leaned in to kiss me again. This time I did not resist and my arms wrapped around her sexy body and I pulled her in close to me. She moaned into my mouth as our tongues wrestled more aggressively this time. She pressed her body in to mine and could feel my growing excitement as she ground her hips into mine. She moved her hands to my shirt to pull open the buttons as we continued our fervent kiss, about half way down she lost patience and pulled the shirt up out of my pants and ripped the last few buttons open.

She pulled back from the kiss and said, "Sorry about that, I'll get you a new shirt. Oh, and fair is fair." She reached behind her and undid her bra, letting it fall to the carpet and revealing her amazing breasts to me.

"No worries, beautiful," I assured her then started kissing her again, my right hand instinctively reaching for her left breast as my left pulled her waist into mine.

Again, she moaned into my mouth as our tongues sought each other out. Her hands now went to my belt buckle and mine to her toned and tanned bottom, kneading the fleshy globes with my hands and loving the feel of her body against mine. Her hands were cool and sent chills across my skin as the back of her knuckles pressed into my abdomen in her frantic quest to open my pants. It was my turn to moan as she finally opened the belt and my pants button quickly after. Even more impassioned than I was, my sweet high school crush turned assertive business woman and adult seductress quickly snuck her hand inside my pants and found my passion for her.

As she grasped me in her cool but quickly warming hand, she broke our kiss and then she proceeded to kneel and quickly peeled my pants down my legs like skinning a banana. She pulled my undershorts with the pants, which left me 'bobbing' in front of her with anticipated excitement. She looked at my excitement then looked up at me.

"Oh my, John, I wished I'd have done this years ago," she whispered as she stood up and kissed me, holding me tightly against her. Everything that had passed since high school…everything…seemed irrelevant as her mouth engulfed mine and her body pressed against mine sent years-long awaited sensations through my muscles and bones.

The feel of her cool hand on my back and her equally warm mouth had me moaning in pleasure, which only seemed to inspire her more. Holding her close and kissing her excited me like no other encounter I'd had before. She was not my first lover, to be sure, but she was my unrequited first love and this moment of passion we were sharing was pure magic that somehow re-connected the years between now and our lives from years earlier.

I was trapped in a way, unable to resist the urges that had been unsatisfied for so many years. I couldn't stop her if I wanted to; and I was pretty sure that I didn't want to, at least in that moment. My mind blazed with passion for her and the sensations she was causing me. I was almost afraid to move, not wanting to do anything to interrupt her as her hands moved over my body. My hands moved across her as

60

well, with minds of their own, exploring her flesh with eager caresses as we stood kissing.

"You taste so dammed good," she professed as she took my head in her hands and kissed me again deeply, sharing her passion for me with her fervor. I kissed her back just as passionately, wrapping my arms around her and pulling her in close to me in a tight hug. It was strange, as I look back on it, as mentally stimulating as my afternoon with Charlie had been; being with Kelly for the first time was anything but mental. I was immersed in emotions and physical sensations, not thinking about what we were doing or the 'right' or 'wrong' of it.

"Lay down" I told her and spun her around to fall back on the couch I had been sleeping on.

"Oh, John yes, please…" her voice trailed off as I kissed her face, her neck and started trailing kisses down her body. My heart pounded and desire flooded my heart as I took in the sight of her laying there. I was drawn to her body uncontrollably and my hands and mouth could not keep from touching and kissing her. I enjoyed the feel of Kelly wriggling underneath me as I did so but the night and our adventure would not end there.

"Oh, hell yes," she exclaimed as she squirmed under my loving touch. I reached down to her pink thong and started pulling it off of her, down across her shapely, tanned legs. She shifted on the couch and moved her legs to help me, both of us eager to take our desires to the next step. I leaned over her and gazed down into her eyes. They appeared to be glassy, glazed over with desire and that only fueled my passion for her more as I leaned in to kiss her again.

She pulled me down onto the couch as we kissed, our now naked bodies lying together. She kissed me hard and deeply and we both shifted our bodies to allow our lovemaking to continue. When our pelvises met, she broke our kiss and looked deep into my eyes. I swear it was like our souls were touching as she spoke.

"This feels so good, John, like you were meant to be with me," she told me between heavy breaths.

"Maybe I was," I quipped, "maybe all of this was just to bring us together, my dear." I leaned down to kiss her again but she put her hands on my chest to stop me.

61

"Don't joke about this, I'm serious," she kept looking into my soul as she spoke, "no one has ever made me feel like I do right now…no one." She added, whispering softly as we moved in unison, "not even Charlie."

The words rang in my ears as we continued our lovemaking. No further words were needed as we let our bodies take over and speak for us. At that moment, I can honestly say that I cared about nothing else. She was all that was on my mind, her body and her kisses invaded all of my senses. All we could do was hold on to each other and share ourselves with each other as our passions took control. Our bodies moved in rhythm and our kisses seemed to blend together into a continuous union of our mouths as we shared the years of our unspoken desires for each other.

After our lovemaking had reached its climax, we finally broke our kiss. She curled up on the sofa, sliding out from beneath me and I squeezed in beside her, holding her tightly from behind. Both of us were breathing heavily and our hearts were still pounding.

"That was amazing," I whispered into her ear, my breath still ragged from our lovemaking; and kissed her softly on her neck.

She gripped my arm with her hand, holding me holding her, and said, "You are amazing. I can't believe it took this long for us to be together."

"Me neither. I just hope it's not that long until the next time," I said, hugging her tighter. I could feel her heart beating as fast as my own under my arms.

"It won't be," she assured me and squeezed my arms around her.

As we lay there together, our hearts and breathing slowly calming down, my mind started thinking about the two of us. I wondered for a bit about how our lives might have turned out differently if I had only had the courage to say something to her all those years ago. I wondered how it could have been if I'd only asked her out on a date or asked her to be my girlfriend instead of longing in silence as I had.

My thoughts then turned briefly to questioning what we had just done, the 'right' and 'wrong' of it so to speak. I couldn't find anything wrong with finally sharing our love for each other. I had no feelings of remorse or guilt, only love and affection for the beautiful woman laying with me on the couch…and thankfulness.

We drifted off into another nap together, curled up in the beginnings of a new love that had just ignited.

Crunching Numbers...

Kelly slept in my arms and I felt as if I knew what heaven must feel like for about an hour or so. I woke up as she got up and gathered up her panties and bra. I watched her lovingly as she put them on and then the robe, letting it stay open rather than covering herself up. I smiled uncontrollably as I watched her, still basking in the feeling of the discovery of new love.

"C'mon, let's see what Charlie's cooking up for dinner," she said to me as she walked over to kiss me again.

"Okay, I'll get up," I told her as she turned to leave. I scrambled to get out of bed and find my own clothes. As I was pulling my pants back up, she paused at the door and looked back with a sly grin.

"Best thing is, now I don't actually have to wear clothes around here," she announced and waltzed out of the room with her robe flying open.

I watched her as she left, marveling at her brazenness. I put the rest of my clothes on except for my shoes and socks and followed her out. The smell of something cooking caught me as soon as I left the bedroom, whatever it was it smelled good. I saw Kelly in the kitchen whispering to Charlie and giggling, so I was certain he was getting whatever details she was giving him about our little escapade together.

"Smells good," I told him, looking in through the opening in the wall.

They both turned and saw that I was back in the room and Charlie pinched Kelly's butt and told her, "Go get dressed for dinner."

She jumped and let out a mock shriek at his pinch, then teasing asked in her pouty voice, "Do I have to?"

"Look darling," Charlie told her, "I know we've both seen you naked but John and I won't be able to keep talking if you are running around naked, so..." His voice trailed off, leaving the rest of his explanation unspoken.

"Fine!" she said in a huff, mockingly upset. "I'll put some clothes on...Chuck." She emphasized the last word and stomped off to get some clothes.

I smiled at the interplay between the two of them; and he was right. She was distracting enough when she was wearing clothes, having her in the apartment half-naked would be far too distracting for me to pay any attention to him. He saw me standing there smiling.

"She only calls me that when she's upset but she'll get over it. There will be plenty of time for us all to play around in between our discussions," he said, adding, "and she'll probably be over here every night now that you two are finally connected."

"Yeah, umm…thanks?" I offered weakly, unsure of what to say to a friend who has just shared his girlfriend with me.

He waved me and that conversation off quickly, as if to tell me he didn't want to talk about it in front of her, saying simply, "Forget about it. You two should be together."

So, I let it go and he went back to cooking dinner. I walked over to the small dinette set with three places set. He had opened a bottle of red wine. I picked it up and looked at the label; it was a modestly priced Merlot. Kelly came back in wearing an oversized t-shirt, probably one of Charlie's.

"Can you boys handle this?" she asked us both. The shirt hung down to about mid-thigh and both Charlie and I agreed that we'd be ok with her wearing it. "Good because I ain't wearing any pants," she teased back and went to sit down and watch television in the living room.

"Okay now," Charlie said to me through the opening in the wall, "go back to the Bible and read Revelations 17, verse 11.

I nodded and turned around, thinking to myself how chaotic living with Charlie was. From one minute to the next it was like being slammed around mentally. One minute I'm immersed in lovemaking and the next minute it's back to Bibles and prophecies. I sighed a bit as I walked over to the huge old book tentatively. It actually intimidated me a bit by this point. I scanned through the pages and found the one Charlie indicated and read it.

"The beast that existed once but exists no longer is an eighth king, but really belongs to the seven, and is headed for destruction."

I walked back over to the opening to the kitchen and said, "Okay?"

"That line is important in that it is one of the very few mentions of the 'eighth' along with all of the 'seven's'; and of course you know what that means, right?" he quizzed me.

"Millennia?" I answered back, a bit unsure if I was following the conversation correctly.

"That's right!" he exclaimed and turned back to the stove, continuing to speak he cooked dinner, "Like I said, it's one of the very few places the number '8' is mentioned in this context; and it does indicate '8 millennia'. One of the very basic concepts that most people don't get is that there were two 'creations of man'. There is the evolution of man, which lasted many millions of years to finally get us to where we were about 6,200 years ago. Then there is the age where we, as a species, gained 'awareness'...awareness of self, life, god and most importantly, time. Mankind did not become a real 'being' until we became 'aware' of ourselves and started using the stars to measure time. That being said, there are two 'stories of man', the archaeological and geological records show the slow passage of time leading up to our becoming aware; the Bible and other religions are the result of the aftermath of becoming aware and learning how to read the stars and tell time."

"Okay, that sort of makes sense, now that you point it out," I responded.

"Now in Nostradamus' book, in the Preface, he quite clearly states that his predictions are perpetual and 'extend from now until the year 3797', which is very important." he turned and used his fingers again as he quoted the text. I walked over to the coffee table and picked up the book and thumbed to the highlighted and sticky-note labeled page. Sure enough, that's what it read.

I walked back over and asked, "And...?" through the opening.

"According to the scientific record as of right now, the oldest calendar that has ever been found or identified is an Egyptian one that dates back to the year 4236 BC. If we take that to be the 'year 1' and add those years to the 3797 AD number, what do we get?"

I pulled out my iPhone and did the quick math: 8,033 years. "Whoa!" I blurted out, "What's with the extra 33 years?" I asked, honestly curious to know what he thought about it.

"Well, that's debatable. It equals one Jubilee Year from the Jewish tradition; and it's also the amount of time that Jesus lived, according to the Church. Plus, it's the concept of 'almost being accurate enough'. I mean, if a hundreds or even thousands of years' old prediction comes that close, I'll spot them the extra 33 for being 'close enough'." He kept wagging his fingers in the air to make quote marks as he spoke, even if he wasn't looking at me.

"There's another way to arrive at the same number, 3797, using Nostradamus predictions and the Bible's reference to sending the beast to the bottomless pit," he said. "Take the year 2001, the year of the attacks and the start of the US War on Terror. Add 25 to that, the number of years Nostradamus said the war would last in another of his predictions."

"Got it," I said to let him know I was keeping up with the explanation on my phone's calculator.

"Add to that the 1,000 years the beast is chained in the pit, the supposed time of peace but the Earth and the US will be busy being destroyed by earthquakes and tidal wave and meteors," he told me.

"Got that too," I replied again.

"Then add to that 771 years," he finished. He offered no explanation for the last number.

I added the numbers and, sure enough, the number 3797 glowed back at me on my iPhone.

"What is the 771 number?" I asked, very curious now.

"Go get the Nostradamus book," he requested. I went in to retrieve it, winking and smiling at Kelly as I interrupted her TV show. She smiled brightly back when she saw me pick up the book. I brought the book back to the opening in the wall.

"Okay, I have it here," I told him.

"Flip open to the Preface where I have my very first sticky note and read the highlighted passage," he instructed.

I did and it was the line about the predictions extending to the year 3797.

"Okay, this is very important because it's the only other date in the book after the year 1792, alongside the 1999 reference. Now, turn the page and read those highlighted sections. You can skip the stuff he's writing to his son," he said.

I did and read through sections 24 through 26.

"Okay, I see a reference to 177 years, 3 months and 11 days in here," I told him.

He stopped cooking and turned the burner off and moved the pan to a cooler spot on the stove. Then he came over to the opening and leaned towards it to talk lightly but with a broad smile.

"This one I am claiming as a victory," he beamed, "That particular line is pure genius by Nostradamus. Read it again, it says 'From this moment, before 177 years, 3 months and 11 days have passed, by pestilence, long famine, wars and, most of all by floods, the world will be so diminished, with so few remaining, that no one will be found willing to work the fields,' and so on. So, basically he's saying that the human race on the planet will be nearly extinguished by then."

"Right," I asked, "but doesn't he mean 177 years from his time?" I looked at Charlie for his explanation.

"No, that's the beauty of it!" he exclaimed and then covered his mouth. I guess he didn't want Kelly to hear. He leaned back in even closer and told me, "Everyone out there, and I mean everyone, thinks that. They speculate on the 1555 date of his book and when he might have actually written the Preface but it's the one and only thing that is 'coded' in the Preface. The genius is that he assigned months and days to it, which are completely meaningless. No, the fact is, he changed tenses on us from speaking in terms of a 1555 person talking to a contemporary to talking backward from the year he just previously identified! So, the time period he mentions is now counting backwards from the 3797 date. How I know this is because the number of years is reversed! He meant that the fields won't be tilled for 771 years before the 'final conflagration'."

"So, once we became aware, we only had 8,000 years as a civilization, no matter how you slice it. Christians, Jews, Hindus, Aztecs, Mayans, and Nostradamus…they knew it all along?" I asked him.

"Exactly!" he explained to me, "and the ancients from every culture have been screaming that at us for centuries now. Take the Hindus and their story of Shiva's dances. In their culture, Shiva represents both our world and the solar system it's in, Shiva does eight dances, all counterclockwise matching the direction our planet and our solar system spins, then rests, meaning after the eight millennia are up, our story is done here on Earth. You know, they even have as part of their religious writings a sequence of time references to relate them to blinks of Vishnu's eyes, a thousand of them in fact, that equates the span of creation to destruction as being about 4.3 billion years. Those writings are over 3,500 years old and their math is pretty accurate. Science puts the world at about 4.5 billion years, so those ancient Hindu's were not far off and to be honest, I'm not sure I trust modern science's measurement as much as the writings of the ancients. Get Kelly, dinner is ready."

I walked over to the futon where Kelly was sitting with one leg crossed. I couldn't help but sneak a quick look at her slightly exposed lap. As I looked up to tell her about dinner, I knew she had caught me looking by the smirk on her face.

"I heard him, I'm coming," she told me standing up and making a point of pulling her t-shirt down. We walked back to the table where Charlie was dishing out the evening's meal.

We all sat down and oddly, Kelly reached out for both Charlie's and my hands and held them. I watched as they bowed their heads and started saying grace. I bowed with them and listened. We all said "Amen" at the end and they started eating.

"Grace?" I asked them both quizzically.

"I say grace before meals and Charlie does too, at least when I'm around," Kelly informed me, turning to wink at him as she did so.

"It can't hurt," Charlie added in between bites.

I tasted the meal and it was fabulous. Charlie was an accomplished cook, if nothing else. "What is this?" I asked him, unfamiliar with the dish.

"My version of Marsala pork chops with pasta and mushroom gravy," he answered back.

"It tastes great!" I complimented him. He nodded approvingly and kept eating. We all basically stopped talking and enjoyed the wine and the food he had prepared for us. Everything was excellent and I was impressed that Charlie knew how to cook and pair the wine so well with the food.

"It's in my recipe book," he offered as he finished his plate and got up to put his dish and silverware in the sink. He came back to the table and sat with us as Kelly and I kept eating.

"Did you ever read that book I gave you called *The Celestine Prophecy*?" he asked me.

"Is that the green book that talked about coincidence and the Mayans a lot?" I answered, taking another bite from my plate.

"Yes, there's a lot more to it but at least you recognize it. There is no such thing as coincidence by the way, or rather, coincidence is how God talks to us individually and collectively. Like how Kelly came into the bar the other night just as you were going to leave. That was intended to have meaning and now, as you can see, it did. It brought you two together and you here to me."

I looked over at Kelly and she made a kissy-face at me as she sat between me and Charlie. I winked back at her playfully and she smiled.

He went on, "So, according to my calculations, Nostradamus and Revelations all indicating we are over 6,000 years into an 8,000 year story; add to that the fact that the ancients identified 88 constellations they use for Astrology, 12 of which earth passes through on its annual orbit. If you could watch the Earth move around the Sun from a distance, its path of travel looks like a huge number eight. That's a LOT of coincidence, if you ask me."

"Gentlemen, when two separate events occur simultaneously pertaining to the same object of inquiry, we must always pay strict attention." I quoted as a response, indicating that I understood what he was saying in a playful way.

"Excellent! A *Twin Peaks* quote," Charlie praised me. "That's very good and exactly the type of understanding of Synchronicity that Jung and Redfield intended. People always say, 'show me a sign' but the signs are all around us, constantly. We just have to learn to see them properly and try to figure out what they mean. As Schiller once put it, 'There is no such thing as chance; and what seems to us merest accident springs from the deepest source of destiny.' And he was right."

He went on, "So, getting back to the numbers, even though modern science and religions don't really allow for Astrology and Numerology, they are required to decipher and understand these predictions, separate from the morality based messages that make them prophecies. Every 2,000 years, roughly, the 'Age' we are in changes as the astrological sign that the Sun rises in changes. You hear people talk about the Age of Aquarius, right?"

"Right," I answered quickly.

"That's what they are referring to, the sign that the Sun is in, and even that has meaning," he explained, "When civilization 'dawned' and man became aware of himself and the greater scheme of things we were in the Age of Taurus, which explains why so many ancient cultures have bull-like symbolism in their belief systems, like the Hebrews, Egyptians, and especially the Hindus who still will not eat beef to this day. When Christ's time came, roughly 2,000 years later, we were just about to enter, the Age of Pisces. That is why one of his famous symbols is a fish, not just because of the 'feeding the multitudes' story but because his coming marked the entry into the Age of Pisces. Most people don't know that but, it has been proven that in Christ's time and for years after and centuries before him, 'wisdom' meant 'knowledge of the stars'. Hence, the three Wise Men from the Christmas tale…they weren't just smart guys and they didn't just follow one star; they followed the stars, a particular constellation that was in conjunction with two planets at the time. That constellation was Aries, meaning the birth happened in the Spring, not Winter, and the two planets were Jupiter and Saturn."

Kelly quietly got up and started clearing the table of hers and my plates as Charlie went on.

"Now back in those days when this stuff meant more to people than it does today. Aries was the sign for Israel, which is quite the coincidence, considering that Israel's Passover and Day of Atonement always included sacrificial lambs and on top of that Christ is called repeatedly the 'Lamb of God'. You see, it's because Aries was Israel's sign and he was born under sign is part of the reason that the phrase is used. Now Jupiter is considered to be the 'God of gods' both as a mythical or religious figure and as a planet being by far the largest. Jupiter was in the head of Aries, indicating a new king was coming, and on one particular date, there was a Lunar eclipse of Jupiter after which Jupiter emerges as they new 'morning star'. That meant that the potential coming of a new 'king of kings' was coming, most likely in Israel. That's what the Wise Men were following, hoping to find the child by the night of the eclipse…which happened on April 17th in 6 BC according to my calculations. Which means the Gregorian calendar is a bit off, by the way."

"That's very interesting," I told him as Kelly brought two beers and set them down in front of us without us asking, noting that our wine glasses and the bottle were all empty. She didn't say anything, she just winked at me and looked at Charlie with a smile; and then went back to the living room to watch the television.

"Isn't Mercury normally called the 'morning star'? I asked, as I had seen something about that somewhere.

"Yes, normally," he explained, "but on that particular day the re-emergence of the 'king of planets' from eclipse was much more significant but a morning that had both Mercury, as the messenger of the gods, and Jupiter, the king of gods, both being 'morning stars' on the same day was, again, too much coincidence for the Wise Men, and for me too."

"Me three," I responded thoughtfully considering his arguments.

Kelly came back with a neatly rolled joint and handed it to Charlie saying, "Here, you guys are going to need this." Then she went in to Charlie's bedroom.

Charlie told her, "Thanks sweetie!" as she left.

He lit the joint, took a big hit, and then passed it to me. I took it from him and we repeated the ritual of smoking and passing. Kelly came back out fully dressed and took the doobie from Charlie and took a quick pull on it, handing it back to me. We both watched her expectantly as she tilted her head back and held the hit in. Finally she straightened up and exhaled, the muscles on her face clearly relaxing as she did.

"I'm out of here guys," she told us, "I got you your first beers and a doobie; you'll have to fend for yourself the rest of the night."

"You're leaving?" Charlie and I asked at the same time.

She giggled at that, saying "you two are talking and don't need me hanging around and interrupting you. Besides," she winked at me as she spoke, "I got what I came for!" She smiled and walked over to Charlie and kissed him goodnight. Then she did the same for me, telling us as she was leaving. "Mmm, a girl could get used to this."

We watched the door close and listened to the sound of her Mustang firing up and her tires chirping as she left the parking lot. With her gone and the joint finished, it appeared I was in for another long night alone with Charlie. Then I pulled out my iPhone and did some quick math.

"If I add up the years based on what you are telling me, we are only at 6,246 years right now...how do you get that we are in the 7th millennia?" I asked him, genuinely curious.

"Great question!" he coughed through his exhale and got up to go to a flip chart page hanging on the wall with the same timeline we were talking about on it. I followed him over and looked at the chart.

"It's the way we count, dude. We start everything at the number '1'. The Egyptian calendar I use for year '1' is from 4236 BC, the Judeo-Christian tradition puts the year '1' at 3761 BC, which is most likely the year Nostradamus used; as the Egyptian calendar was not found until centuries after he lived and he was a Jew that converted to Catholicism during the Spanish Inquisition. Using those two dates you can say, in general, that sometime around the year 4000 BC is when the different races of man became 'aware'. Using that as our counting start, from 4000 BC to 3000 BC is millennia number one, 3000 to 2000 BC is millennia number two, and so on until you get to the year 2000

AD which marked the end of millennia number six; and January 1st, 2001 was our entry into millennia number seven which will last until the year 3000 is over. As you can see, between 3000 and 4000 AD is millennia number eight...but it doesn't get to finish, at least not here on Earth according to those two books and a bunch of other sources."

"I see," I said, "very interesting." It did all seem to make some sort of sense and Charlie definitely could give you his source for any of the information he talked about. He was very well researched. We both stared at his chart for a moment or two more then I went to sit back in the armchair that basically was 'my chair' at this point, thinking about everything we had gone through so far, piecing it all together in my mind. Charlie went back to the kitchen and got us fresh beers while I sat and waited.

"Okay," I said as he returned to the room, set down our beers and sat on the futon, "but we're still waiting on that first prediction to finish, right? So, what else do you have proven? Didn't you say you had Putin by name in Nostradamus' book?"

He took a long drink of his beer, set the bottle down and reached for his special rolling tray.

"Another great question!" he said as he started making another joint for us.

Fire and brimstone...

"Okay," Charlie said looking up and licking the end of the rolling paper to complete the joint, "let's go back to the basics a bit. Open up Nostradamus' book and check out the quatrain in Century six, number 97."

He pushed the heavy book laden with sticky notes towards me and I picked it up and read the passage.

Quatrain number VI-97 reads, in English:

"At forty-five degrees the sky will burn,
Fire to approach the great new city;
In an instant a great scattered flame will leap up,
When one will want to demand proof of the Normans."

"Now a lot of people have wasted a lot of time arguing this particular prediction with regards to the 9/11 attacks but it has nothing to do with that day. Looking at the quatrain as a whole, it is talking about a fire. This fire is near a city that is located on or very close to the 45th Degree of Latitude. The fire starts very quickly and, in some way or another, the French or Belgians are involved with it. To me, that is not a 'vague' prediction, as the critics of Nostradamus would have you believe. In fact, it is quite specific with regards to what kind of disaster he is talking about, the relative location of the fire, and a mention of some of the people involved with the fire. It is interesting to note that, although the four lines are to be considered together, the quatrain sort of repeats itself by declaring the fire twice, in line 1 and line 3."

"So what is it about then?" I asked.

"Right," he went on, "using the same methods as before, and considering the quatrain as a whole, taking into account all four lines, etc.; we get that there will be a fire somewhere on the 45th Parallel Latitude that can be seen in the sky, the fire will be near and approach, or come closer, to a city. This city will be 'new' in some way from Nostradamus' perspective, the fire will start very suddenly, instantly leaping up, and because of this fire, someone is demanding proof from the French and/or Belgians, probably of their involvement in the fire and its cause. The Normans, or rather Normandy, at the same time can

77

refer to either France or Belgium, since they were both at one time part of the greater French empire known as Normandy."

"Okay, I'm following you," I told him, eager to find out where he was heading with this explanation.

"Because it talks about fire and the sky burning and says 'great new city', every time something happens in New York, people run to this prediction. But that's not how Nostradamus works and New York is on the 41st degree of Latitude, so that's too far off to be right. Once a quatrain is figured out, labeled and identified, you can't use it again…it's out of the deck, and you have to move on to the next one. It is my firm belief that if you figured out his predictions, you could map them one-by-one to prophecies in the Bible, most notably the books of Revelations, Ezekiel and Daniel and some others with apocalyptic prophecies in them."

"So what is this one talking about?" I asked again.

"History tells a well-documented tale of a fire that matches the descriptions in this quatrain and has for some time now. In Halifax, Nova Scotia in 1917 there were two ships, the Mont Blanc and the Imo, which collided and caused a huge explosion. The resulting fire killed hundreds of people and destroyed a large section of the city. Halifax was not founded until 1749; making it a 'new city' relative to Nostradamus' time and it lies very close if not directly on the 45th degree Latitude. The two ships involved in the disaster were French and Belgian. The term 'Normans' as a nickname could apply to either of these two countries, considering they are right next to each other and both countries fell within the French Empire at the time of Nostradamus. There it is, quite specific and quite accurate - a prediction of a fire approaching a city at, or near, 45 degrees where the French and/or Belgians are involved. In this case, both were involved, again making the dual meaning of the term 'Normans' is another classic example of Nostradamus' word play."

"So, what does this have to do with the Bible?" I quizzed him.

"Well, to be honest, I've got this quatrain tied to an actual event that happened but I haven't mapped it to a Bible verse yet," he confessed, "but the historical significance is in that, from Nostradamus' perspective the lines between World War I and II are blurred, with the first war setting the stage for the second 'Antichrist', who was seen by Nostradamus as Hitler, to rise to power. This event occurring near the end of World War I has some historical significance somehow to that taking place. Not to mention it happened less than two months after the Fatima visions were finished in October the same year. While I can't 'prove' where it's mentioned in the Biblical prophecies yet, I can prove that it has nothing to do with New York or 9/11."

"True enough," I replied, "now where's Putin?"

"Right, now flip over to Century number two and read quatrain number 28" he directed, and I followed, skimming through the pages to find the prediction he was talking about.

Quatrain number II-28 reads, in English:

"The penultimate of the surname of the Prophet
Will take Diana for his day and rest;
He will wander far because of a frantic head,
And delivering a great people from subjection."

"Now, the first line is the hardest to work through because it contains the 'gist' of this prediction," Charlie explained, "lines 3 and 4 are barely giving any detail at all but line 2 supports my interpretation of line 1. The word 'penultimate' is key here, meaning 'next to last' or 'almost last' or, as I read it, 'the last two' or 'next plus last'. Meaning that as I read that first line, the person being talked about has the same last name as the last two syllables of the name of a famous prophet, presumably one connected to the same country as the leader being identified by Nostradamus here."

"Yes, I suppose I can see that," I listened as I read the footnotes and compared the translated wording to the original on the opposite page.

"That being said," He explained, "to my knowledge, there has only ever been one world leader 'of a great people' whose last name matched a historical figure known for making predictions...ever."

Suddenly, like a light switch had been turned on in my head, I knew the answer. "Putin and Rasputin!" I blurted out.

"Exactly," he confirmed my guess, "and to cement this notion, in the second line 'Diana' as a day of the week means Monday, and the Russian Orthodox Church that Putin is a member of..."

I didn't let him finish, as again I already knew, "...takes Monday as their day of rest."

"Right!" Charlie confirmed my interruption and lit the joint he had been holding all of this time. As he exhaled and handed it to me he added, "He rose to full power as President of Russia in May of 2000 and was in office at the time of 9/11. There were a few little-noticed news reports that came out in November 2001 where they mentioned he was taking time off because of the traveling he'd been doing in response to 9/11 and his own country's fight with the terrorists. The fact that Nostradamus goes out of his way to name him, with little else in the prediction of value, makes me think he's not done yet. I mean, he was President when 9/11 happened but he's out of office already. However, I think by this quatrain going to great lengths to simply identify him that he may have something to do with the Soviets re-forming and starting the empire up again. Besides, he's already announced that he's running for President again in 2012."

"Hmm," I grunted in response and passed the doobie back his way.

I got up to go to the bathroom, leaving Charlie to smoke alone for a bit. I stopped to look in the mirror as I struggled to find the greater meaning behind the things my friend was telling me. Shaking my head and looking away, I walked back to the kitchen feeling defeated somehow, and got two fresh beers out of the refrigerator. I set the beers down on the table between us and took what was left of the joint from Charlie.

"Thanks!" he said and took a drink of his beer. "Take a look at Century ten, quatrain number 66."

Again, I flipped through the pages to find the verse he wanted me to read.

Quatrain number X-66 reads, in English:

> "The chief of London through the realm of America,
> The Isle of Scotland will be tried by frost;
> King and "Reb" will face an Antichrist so false,
> That he will place them in the conflict all together."

"Wow. That seems pretty close to the international reaction following the September 11th attacks," I said.

Charlie explained, "Considering the range of responses from countries around the globe, the efforts by Britain's Prime Minister, Tony Blair, in the weeks following was as vigorous as any American pursuits. Interesting also is Nostradamus calling Mr. Blair the "chief of London" rather than the King of England, which would have been more appropriate for his day and age. The mention of America is widely accepted to be just that by most scholarly experts of Nostradamus' works. The actual French term he used was *par regne l'Americh* which most correctly translated would read, 'the realm, or regime, of America.'"

He went on, saying, "Forgetting the arguments that will undoubtedly be raised questioning every tiny detail of his work, let us consider that Nostradamus was accurate. I cannot imagine a more fitting 16th Century description of Britain's involvement in the War on Terror since the day of the attacks on the US, alongside President Bush's own actions. The almost slang usage of 'King and Reb' by Nostradamus show a clear insight into the nature of the peculiar relationship between Britain and the America's, considering the Revolution and all."

"True, I can see that," I replied, keeping up with his reasoning easier now.

Charlie continued, "The final piece of this quatrain to be considered provides even more support for this being the accurate interpretation: 'The isle of Scotland will be tried by frost.' Taking into account the fact that putting this part of the prediction into the same year or time period could mean the winter of 2000/2001 or the winter of 2001/2002 for Scotland. The latter would seem to make more sense, considering that the winter following the September 11th attacks was colder than the one that preceded them. Take a look at these."

He passed me two pieces of paper, printouts of Internet news articles from the British Broadcasting Corporation. I read them both:

> February 2001 (BBC) – Big Freeze Chaos in North – "Heavy snowfall and gales have left thousands in Scotland and Ireland without power - and are threatening to wreak havoc in northern England. An estimated 100,000 homes in Scotland, and 70,000 in

Northern Ireland had no electricity at one point on Tuesday, with engineers struggling to make repairs."

Charlie talked as I read the first article, "That was the winter in Scotland before the attacks occurred."

I flipped the pages and read the second article:

> September 2001 (BBC) – Big Freeze for Britain? – "Britain could be in for a big freeze, with the climate ending up more like central Canada, say scientists studying the world's oceans. They have found evidence that the flow of cold water from the Arctic has decreased by 20% since 1950. If the trend continues, the supply of warm water to northern Europe will decline, bringing a big chill. The last time this happened, in the 11th to the 18th Century, northern Europe entered the Little Ice Age."

Charlie explained, "My research revealed even more reports of blizzard conditions, freezing temperatures, and a terribly harsh winter in Scotland for the early part of 2001. The predictions for the 2001/2002 winter were calling for more of the same, if not a continual decrease to near Ice Age conditions for that region in the years following. This quatrain seems to be an exact match for the days and years after 9/11 for many different reasons. Some so-called scholars have tried to attribute this one to the American Revolution itself or even Oliver Cromwell and the Protestant Reformation; however, I would have to argue that they do not come close to matching Nostradamus' description here more than the beginning of the US War on Terror. For one thing, during Cromwell's time, America was just forming its first colonies as England's property, so there was no 'realm of America' yet. For another, America and England were fighting each other, not helping each other, during the Revolution."

"True enough," I agreed.

Charlie continued, "And the line about 'The King and Reb will face an Antichrist so false' would imply that the US and Britain faced this Antichrist together, not as opposing enemies, so the World War II theory makes more sense, Hitler being an Antichrist of global proportions and the US and Britain did fight together during this war. However, the problem with this is theory is that America did not enter the war alongside Britain at first nor did they enter that war because of

Hitler primarily. America entered that war because the Japanese had bombed Pearl Harbor. Britain along with France had already been in fierce combat with Germany and Italy by the time America had joined in, so the quatrain does not fit that event nearly as well as it does the events on and after 9/11. This interpretation also does not hold up to the line 'The chief on London in the realm of America' as the more accepted view would be that America traveled to Europe to fight this war, not the other way around. In addition, there is less evidence to support the 'Isle of Scotland will be tried by frost' line for the events of World War II, given the weather news from that time period."

"So, assuming you are right…and I can't see why you're not, all things considered," I offered, "then this is talking about Tony Blair's visit to America right after 9/11 when he and Bush stood together against the terrorists on TV?"

"Pretty much," he confirmed, adding, "and identifies Bin Laden as one of the Antichrist's, or 'beasts', for this time period, although it could also be describing Putin, or another person yet to be known, as the leader of the new and improved Soviet empire. There are a couple of predictions I'm still working on that suggest things may get so bad that we may end up at war with England again."

Then he slid the New American Bible on the coffee table over to me. "Want to hear something really freaky? Read Revelation 6, verse 12."

For Charlie to be calling something 'really freaky' was intimidating, considering the scope of our conversations, but I picked the book up and read the passage. It was talking about the sixth seal and an earthquake.

"Now, years and years ago some geologists with a bunch of taxpayer money and too much time on their hands did a survey along a particular fault line that runs through this country, from New Orleans and the Gulf of Mexico all the way to New York City, passing through the Ohio River Valley. In that study it was found that with the enormous amounts of sulfur in the ground, if something ever caused that particular fault line to quake, the resulting spread of sulfur in the atmosphere…"

I interrupted again, "…would turn the Sun black and the Moon red, right?" I knew a little chemistry.

"Exactly," he confirmed my guess and went on, "now here's another theory of mine that relates to a news story that most Americans have already forgotten but still exists as a problem."

"What's that?" I asked, again my curiosity was peaked.

"America's thirst for oil, we are drilling deeper and deeper every day to get it. That leak in the Gulf was over 100 miles deep, for crying out loud. Now, I believe that the pockets of oil that we are drilling for provide hydraulic support to keep the planet's tectonic plates 'cushioned' if you will, and they are being replaced with seawater as the oil comes out. That's their process" he explained.

"Hmm," I mumbled worriedly. I didn't like the sound of that. I knew something about fluids and hydraulics from my time in the Navy.

Charlie continued, "As you know, oil is a non-compressible fluid, meaning its volume can't be shrunk but it can be pressurized to very high pressures."

I nodded in agreement.

"Saltwater, as you also know, is a compressible fluid and is one that easily boils off if the temperatures or pressures get too high, such as in the case of a 100-mile deep drilling spot. That being said, I believe we are going to see that fault line erupt in an earthquake during our lifetimes because we have already removed so much of the hydraulic cushion from the Gulf end of the fault line with all of the drilling going on there. Not to mention the drilling going on all over the world, I honestly believe that man himself is the cause of many of these disasters we are reading about in the Revelation story; and America's addiction to oil may very well be the reason that the planet starts acting up…at least where the earthquakes, volcanoes, global warming, and the rest of it are concerned. Plus, if I'm right and the Russians nuke New York City, well…that fault line will erupt and it will be the end of New Orleans and a lot of other cities along the way too."

"Damn," I shook my head listening. He was right, I'd never thought of that before but from a mechanical engineering perspective, it made sense.

"Remember them talking about shooting a Nuke down that hole in the Gulf?" he asked me.

84

"Yeah, I remember," was my depressed reply. What a nightmare.

"Everyone in the country, hell the whole world, should have come out of their seats when that was on the table! Can you imagine, with the Earth's core being largely Uranium and Plutonium, what would have happened if we bombed our own planet on purpose? Holy Mother of God!" he ranted and then chugged his beer.

I thought about it too. An explosion of that magnitude so far below the Earth's surface could cause a chain reaction that would ignite fault lines and volcanoes all over the world…a disaster of 'biblical proportions' and the equivalent of the human race shooting itself in the head.

"Damn!" I thought to myself. I told Charlie that was it for me for the night, the clock now indicating it was well past midnight. He nodded knowingly at me and turned on the TV, turning the volume down as I walked away. I went to the guest bathroom and brushed my teeth, then went in to the guest bedroom and pulled out the sofa bed, tossing the sofa cushions aside.

I went back to the living room where Charlie was finishing his beer and asked, "pillow and blanket?"

He pointed to the small closet between the bathroom and bedroom. I looked in and saw a couple of pillows, pillow cases, and a comforter. I pulled them all out and tossed them on the bed, then went back out and told Charlie, "good night."

"You too, man," he raised his bottle in my direction.

I went back to the room, shut the door and curled up among the pillows and comforter, my mind now racing with visions of earthquakes and volcanoes and nuclear mushroom clouds.

Preparations...

By the next day, I was almost in a routine: get up, shower, shave, brush my teeth and check emails and Facebook for updates. I would 'like' or comment blankly, answer emails with barely enough thought to make them sound coherent. Then breakfast and start talking with Charlie about the end of the world, hopefully have some time with Kelly. Then enjoy a wonderful meal followed by the stuff of nightmares, and then off to a drunken slumber.

So, I once again found Charlie sitting in the living room when I was ready for the day to begin.

"Good morning," I announced as I came into the room.

"Good morning back," he smiled and looked up from his laptop at me. "There's a sausage McMuffin sitting on the counter for you," he informed me.

I went in and, sure enough, one was sitting there. I got a glass of milk, opened the packaging and hungrily bit into the sandwich. As I chewed Charlie told me, "I think we'll go out today, get some air."

"Okay by me," I replied and took a drink of milk then went back to eating the sandwich.

About the time I was finished and drinking the last of the milk, he shut his laptop lid and stood up. He came over and got his car keys off of the hook on the wall, stating simply, "I'll drive."

We walked out to his car, wearing our sunglasses, of course, to protect us from the blinding rays that always blasted his front door in the mornings. We got in and he got the car moving.

"Anywhere in particular?" I asked.

"You'll recognize it when we get there. We drove for quite some time. He had the windows cracked and the sunroof open and it was a bright, beautiful day out. The music on his radio was turned up loud enough to hear but not too distracting; and I could hear the occasional call of a seagull. It turns out his radio was playing a music mix he had on his mini iPod and an Eminem song came up. He pressed the volume knob on his steering wheel.

"Listen to this, I love Eminem's music," he said and the volume jumped a couple levels until the subwoofer was thumping loud enough to feel it through the seats. The car was really moving and the air was blowing our hair around a little and it felt a bit like old times again. My hand instinctively started tapping to the beat. It was a rhythmic, funny rap called *My Dad's Gone Crazy*, the song Eminem had done with his daughter's voice mixed in.

Besides the usual gay-bashing and crap about drugs and cursing were several mentions, either directly or indirectly, of 9/11and the Bush administration. Charlie really cranked up the volume about halfway through.

"Seriously, listen to this part," he shouted.

Eminem went on about never changing his ways, the there was a line about, 'more pain inside of my brain than the eyes of a little girl inside of a plane aimed at the World Trade' and then he actually admitted that he doesn't let his own daughter listen to his music. I chuckled to myself at that part.

Charlie paused the iPod and spoke, "He speaks the truth you know. He may very well be a messenger of God in his own strange way."

"What?" I reacted in near shock and I'm sure the look on my face echoed my reaction.

"He does say in quite a few songs lines like, 'God sent me to piss the world off' and 'God sent me here to annoy your little four year old boy or girl' and things like that," Charlie explained. "Did you hear that last part about the little girl aimed at the World Trade Center?" he asked.

"Yeah," I answered, a little irritated that he had to bring 'the discussion' into everything we talked about.

"That line gives me chills because it reminds me of one of the Nostradamus predictions I've been able to nail down for the 9/11 attacks," he answered, looking quite serious, "I'll show you when we get home."

"Weird," I said, not knowing what to say to that.

"And if what he says about the pain in his mind is true, he could be being 'tormented' by the inspirations that come to him when writing these songs of his. In fact, if you get past the vulgarity and violence and drugs, most of his songs are like extremely filthy sermons describing how screwed up life is growing up with drug abusing, irresponsible parents in a crappy society with no cemented belief system; and the effects of extreme use of drugs and alcohol. He screams at us that the things we are doing in modern America are tearing our children's minds apart and ruining out culture. 'The democracy of hypocrisy' he calls us; and he always sings the truth…or at least the truth from his perspective anyway. Yes, he's probably the most violent, vulgar, wasted and angry person spewing venom out there; but the messages he is trying to get people to understand are really closer to what Billy Graham talks about than anything else. Plus, he was the first artist to come out and openly challenge Washington and the government and the Patriot Act, unlike that Toby Keith crap. That song *White America* is genius."

"Well, I'll give you that. Most of his raps are about him and his messed up family life and his screwed up relationships and he isn't afraid to spit on DC, that's for sure; and he does seem very angry," I offered, trying to lighten the tone again.

"You know the songs of his that talk about 'they'll never figure me out' and how his music 'stays stuck in your head for days and days'?" he asked.

"Sure," I chuckled back, curious now as to just how much thought Charlie had put into Eminem and his music.

"I found out a bit about that too," he explained. "You know that song *Kill You*? Here, find it on the iPod," and he handed the small device to me. I flipped back through the menus to Artists and found Eminem, then scrolled through the list of songs and found it. I tapped on it to play it and the song started in the car.

"Listen to the base melody," he told me. I listened, interested in what point could be made by this.

Eminem was rapping about his mom and cocaine and hitting women, and then the chorus started.

"Listen closely," Charlie said and turned the volume up again.

The song rang out, "You do not want to fuck with Shady, 'cause Shady will fucking kill you…" The melody was very specific and simplistic running behind his violent description of killing his wife in the woods and then the chorus came up again.

"Okay, now stop that song," Charlie shouted over the music while lowering the volume.

I paused the song and looked at him expectantly.

"Now go to my playlists and look for the Classical Music folder," he instructed me. I did and looked up at him again.

"Now play the one called *Sarabande and Variations No. 3 from Suite No. 11*. The artist will be labeled 'Handel'," he said.

I found the song and pressed to play it. I could not believe my ears. A piano was playing the same melody as was in the Eminem song! It was the exact same melody, in fact. I looked over at Charlie in shock.

"How the hell did you figure this connection out?" I asked, now very curious. Handel was considered to be a Baroque master and, as a training consultant, I knew that Baroque music had been studied and was found to be the best music to accompany a training curriculum in an accelerated learning, multimedia program. The music skewed as being the best to help new information get more quickly into a person's mind.

Charlie saw me thinking and he knew that I knew the significance of Handel's music.

"Pretty freaky, huh?" he asked, chuckling at me.

"Yes, I will have to admit, even with all of the other stuff you've told me that is freaky. I'll never hear his music the same again, ha, ha!" I laughed back at him. I followed up by asking, "Do you think he does that on purpose?"

"Oh, I'm pretty sure. He's very smart and his references to 'never figure me out' seem to indicate to me that he knows what he's doing. He could very well be using those Baroque and other classical melodies to help push his venom further into the minds of his listeners more easily, which of course makes the songs easier to remember and sells more CD's. At least sometimes, not all of his songs are like that. In fact, this is the only song of his I was able to match up exactly so far; but it made understanding some of his other songs a little easier," Charlie rationalized.

"You know," he continued, "some people did a study in 2000 after he and Brittany Spears both got famous following the 1998 Mtv Spring Break. They found that, for kids in their teens and still in their school years, more of the kids who listened to Eminem were found to respect curfews, be home on time, do their homework and go to school. The kids who listened to Brittany were more likely to be drunken sluts who skipped school. It goes a long way towards proving that old 'spare the rod, spoil the child' message."

I looked out of the windows of the car, we had driven far enough that I knew where we were. He pulled his car into the parking lot of a restaurant on Clearwater beach. We got out and I followed him through the place to the outside tables. He found a table looking out over the ocean and we sat down. He looked at the water while we waited for a waiter. Eventually one came and we ordered two beers, and then just sat thinking to ourselves in the sun.

The waiter came back with our order and set the cans down along with chilled mugs. Charlie thanked him and tipped him well, saying, "Give us a few minutes, please."

"Of course, sir," the waiter said and sped off.

I picked up my beer, poured it into the mug and took a hesitant sip, waiting for the next nugget of wisdom from my friend.

"I'm serious about you and Kelly, you know," he started.

I interrupted, "What is it with you and this thing about me and Kelly?"

He shifted to look at me directly. "I've got this feeling," he confessed to me, "a feeling that something may happen to me soon."

I started to interrupt again and he raised his hand, stopping me.

"I don't care what you have to say about me and my feelings, they are mine and I live with them every day," he stated firmly, "but when that time comes I want you to know that Kelly would marry you; and that I am leaving her everything I have money-wise, of which there is quite a bit still leftover from my Dad's insurance policy. I want you to marry her, sell off all of our expensive sports cars and get a mini-van or something easy on gas and I want you two to move to the East coast and get a big boat to live on…one big enough to get to the Bahamas or further. Sell everything you don't need and be ready to run to sea if necessary to avoid nuclear war or hurricanes or earthquakes or whatever. You'll be safest on the open seas if everything does go to hell around here."

At first I was smirking but as he continued, I could see he was dead serious, "You've done your family tree, right?" he asked me.

"Yes, I have," I said proudly, "I've traced back to two different grand-daughters of Noah, actually."

"That's what I'm talking about," he said, "I don't know my family history at all and because of the things I am doing, I'm probably never going to have kids. But you, see…you and your offspring are probably in the Book of Life, if it comes down to that part of the prophecies being true."

"How could I possibly have kids, knowing what you've told me," I shot back.

"Because your line is one of the one's who will be saved if I'm wrong about the religious implications of these predictions," he explained. "Your line will be taken to the 'new city' and taken off the planet before the rest of it dies completely."

"Are you saying that you believe the moral parts of the Bible now as well as the events themselves?" I asked a bit shocked.

"For now, I will maintain my stance that the events are the events and, since many religions and cultures have identified pieces of this puzzle, that no single one of them is completely 'right' about everything…however, if and when something happens to me, and if the circumstances of how it happens freak you and Kelly out, you know…'coincidences'; then I want you to run to my apartment and clean it out for me. Get rid of the books, papers, charts, my porn, the drugs and anything that would upset my mom. You and Kelly take the rest of that crap out and burn it."

"Okay, man," I assured him, "I'll make sure to take care of all of that."

"Be nice to my mom, let her have any personal stuff of mine she wants but please don't let her see my research or the other stuff. It would really freak her out," he confided.

"Sure thing," I told him again, hardly believing my ears.

"And I mean what I say about Kelly, take her away from here, marry her, have kids, get a boat…seriously," he nearly pleaded at me, "and take my guns, you might need them. Sell your stock and buy gold too."

"Damn, dude," I muttered. He was really making me concerned with all of that talk.

"You know, I was a Christian at one time but then," he offered, "then there was just too much crap my church couldn't explain, so I went searching for my own answers. I found bits and pieces of the truth everywhere, the Aztecs, Mayans, Hindus, and Hebrews, the Norse and Greco-Roman mythologies and stories, the Egyptians, Sumerians…everywhere. Now, I don't know what to believe but if I'm right about something happening to me in a freaky way, that's God talking directly to you and Kelly to straighten up and fly right."

"Well," I answered back, "with my family tree, I could go Methodist, Catholic, Celtic or Jewish, since that's the progression my ancestors went through, arguably. Which one do I choose?"

"If I get stricken down in such a way as it has some kind of meaning, I'd suggest Catholic to be on the safe side," he answered, adding, "and write a book."

"What?" I questioned back, wondering what this new request of his was.

"I've never written any of this stuff we are talking about down, except for my notes and charts and stickies, so I'm saying if something happens to me, write a book. Maybe you'll make some money from the controversy or just use it to teach your kids what's going on in the world around them. Just please, you are a writer; and be as detailed as possible. Write about everything that's happened to you since you got here, everything we've talked about."

"Well," I explained, "I'm a technical writer; you know procedures and processes and stuff like that. But I'll give it a try if that's important to you."

"It is," he said simply but seriously.

With that he finished his beer and signaled for the waiter to come over. I thought long and hard about what he had said. I guess he was right, with as much as he'd told me so far, if something really weird happened to him, I'd be scared out of my mind, to be honest. I wasn't sure how Kelly would react, devastated most likely. As I thought about all of this, I wondered at the fact that this all started out as a weekend getaway to see some old friends. Now it had turned in to one of the most serious trips I could have ever made and I was committed to doing a lot of serious things for Charlie at this point.

He ordered another round and we just sat there for awhile, looking out over the ocean.

Random Acts...

Eventually the sunny day grew shorter and the wind got cooler and Charlie and I had sat for quite awhile in silence. I was happy that we didn't talk about much more than we had. We just sat and drank and watched the tide roll in, each absorbed in our own thoughts for a time. I watched as the seagulls flew across the water in search of fish and remembered Charlie's explanation of the world moving from Pisces to Aquarius. That song by The 5th Dimension came to mind, they sang so happily about it..."little did they know," I quipped in my head.

I looked down at the table and saw that, between us we had killed a six pack and done a little damage to the sampler platter of appetizers that Charlie had ordered. Not a bad day at the beach, the end of the world notwithstanding. I was finishing my beer when Charlie got up and walked back to where the waiter was. He came back as I set my empty mug down.

"I took care of the tab," he said, "let's head back home."

"Fine by me and thanks for lunch," I said standing up.

"Not a problem," he replied and we headed back to the restaurant to go to the parking lot. I followed him out and we got back in his car to head back to his apartment.

Once we got back on the main road, Charlie started talking again, "You know, the messed up thing about people is that they focus on the differences in things and can't see past them to find the commonalities."

"How so?" I asked back.

"Like when people argue over religions, or science and religion, or science and mysticism or any of that...they focus on the differences like, 'my Bible says we were created in seven days' and the others respond, 'well the scientific record says it took billions of years' and both parties go away mad at each other. There's no need for it, really."

"How do you mean?" I queried, again curious as to what he was trying to say.

Charlie explained, "Okay, let's take evolution's side for example. For those who do not believe the warehouses of archaeological evidence that support Darwin's theory and the proof that exists in front of their eyes on this planet even today, then they should at least allow themselves to think, 'Well, what if Darwin was right?' So, let's assume that Darwin was right, as his arguments are valid and the proof he and the historical record present to support his theory are overwhelming. If Darwin was right, and evolution is the process of change that brought the plants and animals on this planet to their current state, does that then mean that the Creation story is wrong; or that there is no Creator? No." He answered his own question and went on as I listened carefully.

"One theory being right does not necessarily mean any other theory about the same subject is wrong. This ridiculous battle between science and religion over 'Creation vs. Evolution' is completely unfounded. One theory being correct does not automatically exclude other theories. The examples to prove this are too many to mention them all. They can be found in science and any other aspect of the world at large. Take Einstein's Theory of Relativity for example, just because he defined a relationship between energy and matter does not mean that is the only equation they are found in or work in. Likewise, it does not exclude the possibility that there is a greater solution that further describes this relationship and expands on it."

"Agreed," I said, nodding my head as he continued.

"So, just like with Einstein's theory, so should Darwin's Theory of Evolution be taken. He has successfully found a piece of truth and shared it with the rest of the world. The purpose of uncovering truths is not to prevent others from searching further, but rather, to spread the word to allow other people to grasp it, understand it, and build on it. To allow for the possibility that there is a greater question with a greater answer that would include and build on his findings. In other words, it allows for the possibility of both Creation and Evolution."

"Okay, I'm listening," I told him, honestly curious and thankful we were talking about something other than death and Hell and curses.

"Taking the Biblical story of Genesis: 'In the beginning God created the heaven and the earth.' From there, the story starts with the Universe as a void, which science agrees with. The next significant act is 'Let there be light; and there was light' very specifically. Again, according to science, before the Big Bang, the Universe was a void, followed by the Big Bang, which released massive amounts of hydrogen and helium and other trace elements into the Universe. 100 million years after that, the huge clouds of hydrogen collapsed in on themselves forming the first stars, which then gave the Universe light. That event is considered by many scientists to be the 'real creation' of the Universe as we know it, rather than the Big Bang itself. I've got a Discover magazine at the apartment from December 2002 that describes the 'Day the Universe Lit Up'."

"Right," I jumped in, "I've seen some Discovery Channel stuff on the Big Bang."

"And it's not just the Jews and Christians either," he went on to say, "there's a Chinese account over 2,200 years old that reads something like, 'Before Heaven and Earth had taken form, all was vague and amorphous'. The Mayans also had in their creation story something to the effect of, 'Where there was neither heaven or earth sounded the first word of God…and all the vastness of eternity shuddered'. These accounts are all in agreement about the universe being a vast void until God created everything, and they are from all over the world and from vastly different cultures. Again, with all these pieces of the truth coming from so many different sources, it's hard to say exactly who is 'right' about everything; but one thing is for sure, if they all agree on that point, then it has to be right in some aspect."

"I think it's interesting that so many different sources all have essentially the same story," I interjected. "It's hard to think we are still arguing over it."

"Exactly," he continued, "so far, science and the Judeo-Christian stories, as well as the Chinese, Mayans and many others, agree with the main difference being in the Bible's use of the term 'days' for the entire event from big bang to the creation of man; but in doing only a little research on the actual wording, the Hebrew term used in the original *Pentateuch* is a term that can be used interchangeably with 'ages' and 'times' and other translations describing various amounts of time. That being said, except for the difference in the amount of time being described, the creation of the Universe is very similar from both scientific and religious sources; and the fact that science can't answer the question 'why' it happened, only approximately 'when' and 'what' happened, then that leaves the question of 'who' wide open."

"So far, I agree with you," I assured him.

He went on, "Continuing with the story from Genesis, the earth is separated from the heavens and then the Sun, Moon and stars were created. Again, science agrees with this for the most part, the actual specific order of the three notwithstanding; but the solar system did come together in the same general timeframe. All of the stars and planets and moons currently in existence were once parts of the tremendously large super-stars that first lit up the Universe then exploded, giving the energy and matter needed to form all of the celestial bodies we see in the night sky today. In fact, everything in existence was once a part of these huge super-stars, including us."

"Hmm," I mumbled as I thought about the idea that part of me was once 'heavenly'.

Charlie kept talking, "Getting back to the Darwinian argument, the Genesis story goes on to say that once dry land formed on the planet, that plant life emerged, which again, agrees with science and evolution. The next lines are very important as they quickly but correctly describe the order in which animal life evolved: 'Let the waters bring forth abundantly the moving creatures that hath life, and fowl that may fly above the earth in the open firmament of heaven.' Again, according to Darwin's theory, after plant life was formed, the first animal life to evolve happened in the oceans, which then evolved to simple animal forms on dry land one of the earliest types being species of birds; albeit after the reptiles, which aren't mentioned separately in the story until the snake appears later on, but the omission doesn't make it 'wrong'. Then, after fish and birds, the story specifically mentions whales, which would rank among the earliest mammals on the planet; again the mammals appearing after the life in the oceans and sky evolved is accurate enough to the evolution theory to keep them aligned."

"I'm with you so far," I said, not finding anything in his explanation I could argue.

He held up a finger as if to make a point, "To expand on my comment earlier about the reptiles and their omission, the fact that the creation story does not address the 'Age if the Dinosaurs' is another debate about the validity of it. We must remember, however, that the book of Genesis and the four books that followed it were all written by Moses or some other human under his direction. Being human and having never set eyes upon a living dinosaur, there would be no reason to expect them to be included, as they were unknown to most humans until the archaeologists started putting their skeletons back together thousands of years later. Also, considering that they came and went long before the first homo-sapiens appeared, their part of the story is negligible at best, from a 'creation story' standpoint for religious purposes."

"But it is a pretty glaring omission," I countered.

"The real irony, in my opinion," he countered back, "is that the dinosaurs' omission is one of the main arguments against the Creation story but at the same time they are the source of our modern energy needs and are the main reason for the wars and turmoil going on in the world right now. It's almost a visible 'test of faith' that the wars for fossil fuels mark the time of Armageddon and that they wouldn't even exist without the one piece missing from the Creation story that would have made it more believable, had it been included."

"Anyway," he got back to his original discussion, "It is only after the creation, or evolution, of sea life, simple animals and then sea mammals that the Genesis story continues with 'Let the earth bring forth the living creature after his kind, cattle and creeping thing, and beast of the earth after his kind; and it was so.' Again, this pattern mimics Darwin's version in that the land mammals and other species came after the earlier, simpler forms of life evolved into them. After all other plant life and animal life is created, or evolved, the story goes in to the creation of man 'in his own image'. Besides the fact that the commonly accepted time for the creation of the Universe to Man only takes seven 'days,' or more correctly 'ages,' and the dinosaurs; this is the main argument against evolution: that man was created in God's image and not evolved from some earlier animal form. However, this argument is un-winnable because many people are confusing the 'what' and the 'how'. The 'what' in this case is 'man was created in his image' and the 'how' is evolution."

The car swerved as he took his hands off of the wheel to make the quote marks.

"Just drive, dude," I warned him, "I'm following you."

He put his hands firmly on the wheel and continued, "Using a simplified cooking example, anyone could make a gingerbread cookie 'man' in their own image and make that claim. However, someone else could come along later and identify the process of mixing the ingredients, forming it and baking it as 'how it was evolved' and that its origins are flour and water. Both statements are still true, the first describing 'what happened' and the second describing 'how it happened'. Applying that back to the question Darwin, society as a whole should come to terms with the fact that evolution does not conflict with the idea of creation; it merely gives us more scientific detail on how may have been accomplished; and stop fighting about it."

"You make a good point," I agreed, "If we could just get science and the Church working together it would be a lot easier for a lot of people."

"It's not just science and religion either," he added, "In that book *The Celestine Prophecy*, the author offers an incredible viewpoint on the origins of science as it applies to society and religion and history. There are other books and reference works that also describe the same origins, however, Mr. Redfield gave a description that not only tied in those references and resources but explained it in a way 'that just made sense.' The basic, boiled-down idea presented there is that modern day science has its roots in mysticism and religion. In addition, science was developed originally to prove the works of God...not to dispute them or refute them. The historical record speaks volumes to support these ideas. In ancient cultures, religions were not only in political power, but often the only source of literature and other forms of learning. Religion controlled everything in the earliest days of civilization."

"Okay," I said, quickly gripping the dashboard every time the car swerved as he made his points.

"Likewise, from the Middle Ages on, where we have a somewhat more reliable historical record than with the ancient past, science has evolved out of what are today considered New Age concepts. Alchemy and Astrology being the most significant, they are the basis for much of what is considered 'modern science' now. Although those same modern scientists would have you believe there is no value to those age-old concepts...ironic, isn't it? Alchemy, or the pursuit of turning different materials into gold, provided all of the groundwork for modern day Chemistry, Physics, and other sciences. Likewise, Astrology was certainly the pre-cursor of Astronomy and Astrophysics and all of the scientific pursuits dealing with outer space."

"True, true," I agreed and listened he explained further.

"These are two excellent examples of things you do not have to believe in for them to affect you. No one people on this planet has not been affected by the advances in physics, chemistry, and space exploration, with a very few possible exceptions individually. Even the chemists and physicists do not believe in Alchemy, per se'. However, it is irrefutable that it did have an impact and effect on people's lives even to modern times. Astrology is probably the most impactful, surviving to modern times nearly intact and forming the basis for modern Astronomy. Whether you believe in Astrology or not, it has affected you and everyone else in the world. One easy example is the names of the planets and the days on the calendar. Both are from Astrological, and therefore, mythological, references. Monday is "Moon Day", for instance."

"Right," I concurred and added, "and Saturday is 'Saturn Day' and Sunday is, well, pretty freaking obvious."

"Exactly," Charlie agreed and continued, "Medicine is another field that can be traced backwards to mystical beginnings. Even before the 'sawbones' and barbershop surgeons of the recent past, medicine's roots go right back to religion, if you look far enough. The burning of frankincense, for example, stems from the ancient belief that it would ward off diseases, such as Smallpox. Likewise, the washing of the hands and feet before entering a church can be said to be the earliest examples of sanitation and disease control. Whether priests or shamans or monks, the earliest forms of 'drugs,' used both medicinally and spiritually can be found in their hands. Early witchcraft, and I mean pre-Christian early, besides being a religious belief system that was not associated with the devil originally, it was also the warehouse of knowledge for using different herbs and roots and such to make 'cures'" or potions, some of which can still be found in today's medicines."

"And some can be found in modern day health food shops and some alternative places," I added.

"Exactly," he confirmed, "the second major point is that science was not developed to prove God wrong, rather it was developed to prove how God does things. The Renaissance that occurred following the Middle Ages that brought back to life 'the sciences' was done so by the people at the time to prove God. The stance of modern day science being against God and religion has developed only in the last 500 years or so of civilization. Considering that civilization itself is over 6,000 years old…that is a very, very small percentage of time in comparison."

"Good point," I answered back, thinking about it. "If we could just get everyone to give a little and come together on some of the disagreements, it would go a long way to helping people get along."

"Yeah, I suppose," he argued, "but I don't know. It's like with the Revelation story, I'm not sure if the moral judgments being made are of mortal consequence. I mean, if something comes and knocks the Moon out of orbit or huge earthquakes tear our country apart, then that's what's going to happen. Is changing our ways on Earth as a people somehow going to stop it from happening? I can't imagine so; and if it did, then it would never happen so we'd never know. Luckily, mankind is predictable enough to know that the story will continue to unfold as it was told. Such is the nature of prophesy and prediction."

He continued after a brief pause, "I think whoever it was that may have had these visions simply assigned a moral message to justify why we were suffering so much damage, and laying blame as he understood it given the visions in his head. Nostradamus, on the other hand, only did predictions but since the disaster parts of both stories match up, I think whatever is coming is coming; and even if the entire nation went Catholic overnight, the meteors will still come and the earthquakes will still rumble and the seas will still rise. It kind of makes that one message in the Sermon on the Mount completely meaningless."

"Which one is that?" I queried.

"The one about 'blessed are the meek'," he explained, "I mean what is the point of inheriting the Earth, if He is just going to come back 2,800 years later and destroy it? It's not a great selling point for being meek now, is it?"

"No, I suppose not," I agreed, shaking my head. He made a good point, that's for sure. I thought for a moment then answered him back with a joke.

"Blessed are the cheese makers?" I asked in a fake English accent, recalling a line from Monty Python's movie.

He laughed, a rare sight for Charlie and shot back, "If you call me 'big nose' one more time..." he responded in his own fake English accent. Then he got serious again.

"And another thing," he added, "the book didn't even show up in any bibles until after about 96 AD, so what's up with that? All of the original apostles were already long dead, so if they didn't include it or write it, then who did? And if St. John did indeed write it, why did the original apostles not put it in the book in the first place? Once again, by the church not being forthcoming with this stuff in the first place, they created another mystery that caused more questions than it answers."

"Well, a lot of it does resemble what Malachi and Daniel were talking about in the Old Testament, so at some point both the Jews and Christians will figure out what's going on," I posed to him. I knew a little about the Bible too.

He looked over at me; his face contorted in thought and said simply, "Hmm."

With that he turned up the radio volume a bit and we drove the rest of the way back in silence. When we finally got back and got inside his apartment, he immediately went to his special tray to make us another joint. I went to the kitchen and got a couple of cold one's and came back to the living room.

"Did you need to get in the guest room for anything, check emails, anything like that?" I asked him.

"No, I'm good with my laptop," he said as he licked the paper and put the final twist on the doobie. He lit it, took a big hit and passed it to me.

"Okay, before we get too far gone, show me this Eminem thing you found," I told him and took an equally big hit from the smoldering joint.

He exhaled and leaned over, picking the large book up and thumbing through the pages. He set the book down and slid it towards me.

"Take a look at Century ten, number 82," he told me. I flipped through the pages and read.

Quatrain number X-82 reads, in English:

> "Cries, weeping, tears will come with knives,
> Seeming to flee, they will deliver a final attack,
> Parks around to set up high platforms,
> The living pushed back and murdered instantly."

"Okay, I'm game," I told him, "What do you have for this?"

"Well, you remember that line from the Eminem song, right?" he asked me.

"Sure, seems creepy enough," I answered back, "but I don't get it entirely."

Charlie began, "The quatrain, while seemingly vague, gives a disturbingly detailed insight into the actual hijackings that occurred on that fateful day in September. 'Cries, weeping, tears will come with knives' speaks directly to the stories that the victims on those planes relayed to their loved ones only moments before their doom on their cell phones. The hijackers used only knives and box cutters…no bombs or guns. The flight plans of the planes themselves before the crashes, the history of airline hijackings, and possibly even the lies that the hijackers told the passengers and crew on those flights all seem to fit this line of the quatrain."

"Line 2 says, 'Seeming to flee, they will deliver a final attack' and is an excellent description of what actually happened. Taking over an aircraft and turning it around, seemingly towards the ocean and out of the country as so many other hijacked planes before them, appeared at first as if they were 'Seeming to flee.' Particularly, if that story was given to one of the planes by the hijackers themselves, such as 'We are flying to our homeland' or something similar. Instead of fleeing, however, this band of terrorists never did intend to flee and instead delivered a 'final attack' using those aircrafts. Until that day, most hijackings were used to 'flee' to another country."

"The line that says 'Parks around to set up high platforms' is confusing, to say the least. I can't be sure if Nostradamus was describing the temporary buildings and platforms set up during the rescue and recovery efforts in New York City or if he literally meant the New York City 'parks,' like Central Park, and tall buildings near the area used for tributes, fundraisers and other events after the mess was cleaned up. What is certain, however, that given the context of the other lines of the quatrains and the hijackings they describe, this is certainly the least significant of the four lines of the quatrains for understanding the importance of its relationship with current world events."

He finished with, "The last line is painfully obvious in both its meaning and its delivery. 'The living pushed back and murdered instantly'. I cannot imagine a more accurate description of an airliner full of people smashing into a heavily populated building and exploding on contact. There has not been another satisfactory explanation of this quatrain prior to 9/11 to conflict with this interpretation and quite simply, the detail that is presented in this 16th Century verse are so extremely similar to the tragedies that occurred that day that I can't imagine another set of events at any time in history that involved the use of this imagery in such glaring and chilling detail. The fact that the line in that Eminem song mentions 'the eyes of a little girl inside of a plane aimed at the World Trade' connects the two events for me significantly enough."

"Hmm," I answered in a mumble. I didn't want to agree with him but it was hard not to.

Corinthian leather…

"Take a look at this," he said as he thumbed through the pages of Nostradamus' book again. He found the page he was looking for and slid the book back over to me.

"Remember when I said that each of his quatrains could be mapped to a Bible prophesy?" he asked me.

"Yeah," I answered quickly.

"Read Century six, quatrain number 100," he said, adding, "It's the only one in the whole book with a title and it's Nostradamus' version of the 'curse' I showed you in Revelation 22."

I read the lines, noting that it was indeed titled *INCANTATION OF THE LAW AGAINST INEPT CRITICS*.

> "Let those who read this verse consider it profoundly,
> Let the profane and ignorant herd keep away:
> And far away all Astrologers, Idiots and Barbarians,
> May he who does otherwise be subject to the sacred rite."

"Just like with the Bible, needing the knowledge of astrology and numerology to figure it out; you need a working knowledge of astrology to figure out many of Nostradamus' predictions…so, the clues to figuring out the puzzles are hidden in the 'curses' that come with them," he explained.

"Huh," was my only response, sitting back and thinking. Maybe he was right.

"Now look at this," he said, picking up the book again and shuffling through the pages. Again, he slid the open book over to me. "Check out Century one, quatrain 54," he said.

I leaned over and read the lines Charlie had indicated.

Quatrain number I-54 reads, in English:

> "Two revolutions made by the wicked scythe-bearer,
> Change made in realm and centuries:
> The moveable sign so obtrusive in its place,
> To the two equal and like minded."

"Now look at the footnotes," he instructed, and I did. Line 1 had a footnote that two revolutions of Saturn would take 59 years, and that Libra was the meaning of 'the moveable sign', and that line 4 could also be translated to 'To the two like-minded ones'. I looked up at Charlie, indicating I was ready for his next explanation.

"My take on this is," he started, "that line 1 is not talking about Saturn, unlike Mr. Leoni's note. I take this to mean the two angels in the clouds bearing sickles in Revelation 14 that I told you yesterday were a reference to 9/11. The 'two revolutions' refers both to the two years between the attacks on Russia in 1999 and the US attacks in 2001; and the two 'thrusts' of the sickles that the angels made on 9/11. The 'two revolutions' then would refer literally to two trips the earth made around the sun. Again, this fits with the whole 'dual meanings' thing with Nostradamus. There is no carnage mentioned but the reference to 'change in realm and centuries' in line 2 no doubt are referring to the elections that put Bush and Blair, and Putin for that matter, in office in the time between 1999 and 2001, which occurred along with a change in not only century but also millennium."

He continued, "I agree with Mr. Leoni about line 3 referring to Libra as the 'moveable sign', which to me indicates the figurative meaning of Libra and not necessarily the constellation itself; the figurative meaning being 'justice' or 'the law'. Considering the troubles that Bush and Blair faced in capturing and interrogating the suspects associated with 9/11 and Bin Laden; including civil rights lawsuits, charges of torture and violations of the Geneva Convention…that seems to fit exactly. Considering their mention in that other quatrain, Bush and Blair seem fitting for line 4 as well. As if in support of this translation, Nostradamus once again uses the term 'realm' to identify America, as well as Britain in this case."

"Okay, I guess that works," I replied. I wasn't sold on it but I couldn't find fault with his interpretation either.

"Let's go back to the big book and re-read the part about the angels with the sickles again, to get that imagery fresh in your head," he said as he walked over to the huge old Bible. I followed him over.

He flipped the pages open to Revelation 14, and then stepped away. I leaned down and read about the two angels reaping the bodies of man and causing massive destruction.

"Okay, now let's look at all of the 9/11 predictions I found so far again, in the right order, and maybe it will be clearer to you," he offered, "I know it's hard jumping back and forth like I do."

We went back to sit down and he sounded off the quatrain numbers as I picked up the book on Nostradamus and read.

X-72:

> "The year 1999, seventh month,
> From the sky will come a great King of Terror;
> To bring back to life the great King of the Mongols,
> Before and after Mars to reign by good luck."

"Terror attacks on Moscow, Putin is Vice President, Russia considers using a 'nuclear option in response, the only time marker we have from Nostradamus other than the 3797 year," Charlie said as I read.

II-28:

> "The penultimate of the surname of the Prophet
> Will take Diana for his day and rest;
> He will wander far because of a frantic head,
> And delivering a great people from subjection."

"Putin elected to office as President, foreshadowing his involvement with the US War on Terror," Charlie reminded me.

I-54:

> "Two revolutions made by the wicked scythe-bearer,
> Change made in realm and centuries:
> The moveable sign so obtrusive in its place,
> To the two equal and like minded."

"The two years between the Moscow attacks and 9/11 and reference to Bush and Blair being equals and recently elected during a century change, and including the reference to the 'scythe' relating it back to the imagery of the 'sickle' used in the Revelation story," he explained.

X-82:

> "Cries, weeping, tears will come with knives,
> Seeming to flee, they will deliver a final attack,
> Parks around to set up high platforms,
> The living pushed back and murdered instantly."

"The actual 9/11 attacks from a human perspective," he stated calmly.

X-66:

> "The chief of London through the realm of America,
> The Isle of Scotland will be tried by frost;
> King and "Reb" will face an Antichrist so false,
> That he will place them in the conflict all together."

"America and England working together after 9/11, Blair's visits to the US and holding arms up with Bush together on TV, continuing cold weather in Scotland ever since," he said. "What do you think?"

"I think you are scaring the hell out of me," was my worried reply.

"I think that's the point of it all," he answered back and got up to get a fresh round of beers.

He came back in and set the new beers down and cleaned up the empties, taking them to the kitchen as I sat in bewilderment, shock really.

He brought me out of my shock with a quick statement, "Oh yeah, it's Kelly's turn to cook tonight so I would expect pizza or Chinese food."

Kelly was going to be there soon, which knocked my brain off of the train wreck that Charlie had put it on moments earlier. She was enough to steal my thoughts away from any subject. I looked over at the clock and saw that she could get here anytime soon.

I asked him as he sat down again, "So what's the deal with the Muslims?"

He nervously looked at the clock and said, "Okay but quickly because I don't want to be talking about this part when Kelly gets here."

"Sure thing," I said simply.

He slid the small Bible on the coffee table to me and said, "Read Revelation 2, verse 9 and scan through the rest."

I did and he spoke as I read, "The line about 'I know thy works, and tribulation, and poverty, (but thou art rich) and I know the blasphemy of them which say they are Jews, and are not, but are the synagogue of Satan.' is describing the nation of Islam by using a reference to the fact that the Arabs, when Islam was first formed as a religion in 610 AD, made the claim that they were descended from Ishmael; and in fact Islamic tradition celebrates Ishmael over Isaac, who the Jews are descended from. Both were sons of Abraham, who is considered the Father of Israel, through separate women. The reference to them is as plain as day and is the reason for the Crusades and all of the other crap that's been going on between Christians, Jews and Muslims ever since."

"Huh," I grunted, it did seem pretty obvious once he pointed it out.

"Besides that," he continued, "all of the references to the seven churches and the messages to them in this part of the book talk about how those churches are sitting in places 'where Satan dwelleth'. Well, all of those churches named are located in the country of Turkey, which is essentially…"

"Muslim," I interrupted.

"Exactly," he confirmed, adding, "and consider this: everyone is always talking about 'the Antichrist' as being people in contemporary history; and that's probably Nostradamus' fault because he uses that term in place of 'beast' in his book; but there really was only one Antichrist and that was Muhammad. Besides the fact that Salman Rushdie wrote an entire book on the subject called *The Satanic Verses*, which I highly encourage you to read by the way, it's a perspective thing."

"How do you mean?" I asked him.

"Well, you can only have an Antichrist if you are Christian, right? The Jews do not acknowledge Christ, so they are unconcerned about Antichrist's, if you know what I mean. It's the same with the Hindus, Buddhists, and the rest," he explained.

"I guess so, yeah that makes sense," I answered back.

"Okay then, so from the Church's perspective, to define an Antichrist you'd have to have the following criteria," he said counting with his fingers as he spoke, "First, he or she would have to come after Christ's time; second, he or she would have to claim being equal to Christ; third, he or she would have to refute Christ's divinity; and fourth, he or she would have to establish a religion that became equally as large and/or powerful as Christ's. If you think about it, the only person ever to have lived that fulfills all four of these requirements was Muhammad. Period. His religion has grown to a third of the world's population, notice how that matches how many people will die in Revelation story, and his religion does refute Christ's divinity. Most everyone out there is afraid to say it but I'm not. Muhammad was the original and true Antichrist."

"Whoa," I said in surprise, "That's a powerful claim."

"Prove me wrong," he challenged. I couldn't think of anything to say, so he continued.

"Besides, think about it. If Christianity was the evolution from the Hebrew 'eye for an eye' policy to Jesus' 'turn the other cheek' message, then how could the next evolution go back to 'eye for an eye and kill the infidels while you are at it'? Charlie's fingers waved in the air as he made his points.

"Well, that's true," I said, adding, "and the extremists condone suicide bombings, which is supposed to be quite a mortal sin."

"Exactly," he confirmed, "making people kill themselves under the belief that God will reward them with 72 virgins in Heaven is ridiculous. I mean as badly as Islamic law allows them to treat women on earth and the fact that Jewish law, Christian morals and even Islam does not allow for rampant sexual activity here in this life, how in the world could anyone think that God wants to see a sex orgy like that up in Heaven? The devil himself must bust a gut laughing every time one of them blows themselves up."

"Well, I can't argue with that," I interjected at his pause.

Charlie nodded in agreement and continued, "Besides the fact that those damn suicide bombers violate the commandment 'Thou Shalt Not Kill' doubly, by killing both themselves and their victims; they really don't get what a martyr is. You have to be 'made' a martyr, you can't make yourself one. You have to be killed by someone else for your religious beliefs, not kill others in the name of your religion. They have the whole concept backwards and I believe, ironically, that they are actually creating martyrs of their victims, rather than becoming martyrs themselves. Sure, there are plenty of 'truths' in the Quran but that doesn't mean anything; there are many references in the Bible that indicate the devil can speak the truth as well as lies."

"Huh, I suppose so," I answered weakly, becoming increasingly uneasy with the conversation.

"For another thing, the original name for the Moon was the pagan goddess 'Sin' and it is represented by the metal Silver. The Sun's representative metal being gold. The references in the Bible to 'sin' are many but there is a specific reference in the Revelation story to the 'followers of the false prophet'. Now tell me, which major world religion uses the Moon as part of their main symbolism?"

"Islam," I answered more quickly as the puzzle pieces fell into place.

"Exactly," he confirmed, "and to top it off, when he was preaching his new religion, Muhammad 'squatted' on the Holy Lands purposefully to cause the future turmoil between Israel and their Islamic neighbors. I mean, Jesus was Jewish, that's why he was there and the Christians and Jews get along peaceably enough nowadays; but when Muhammad went to Bethlehem and Jerusalem and the rest, he was just stirring up trouble for the future. He was an Arab, so he had no business in those places other than to tarnish the fledgling Christian religion; and to mess with the Jews."

"That sounds true enough," I said, "I always wondered about that myself. The three-way fight for the Holy Lands is always going to be a problem."

"Not after Armageddon's over," Charlie winked at me chuckling. "Kelly's on her way, so we've got to find something better to talk about now."

"No problem," I told him, very much relieved that he didn't want to talk about this stuff for awhile. Some of what he was telling me extremely disturbing and these last few conversations had really started to work up a sense of doubt over his claim that the morality wrapped around the prophecies had no meaning.

Rather, a growing fear in my mind was that, even as he was explaining his ideas to me, he was revealing that he had more than a little doubt about that himself. His repeated talks about taking care of Kelly if something happened to him and his numerous references to God and the Devil not only revealed that he held some belief in religion but stirred up my own memories of going to church as a youth. I found myself starting to wonder if maybe we shouldn't all take church and religion more seriously in light of what we were talking about.

Kelly's song...

Both Charlie and I scrambled to clean up the apartment quickly, before Kelly got there. It was kind of funny, we were chasing after her like a couple of puppy dogs and she wasn't even in the apartment yet. He was in the kitchen tidying up the mess in there, as if a few empty bottles and a McDonald's wrapper was a 'mess'. I stayed in the living room and carefully piled a few books here and there, moved some piles of paper into neater stacks, being careful not to upset the chaotic organization of them. Charlie finished in the kitchen just as I was finishing what I was doing.

Sitting down, he said, "She must be picking up dinner," offering it to me as the reason she hadn't arrived yet. I shrugged my shoulders as he turned on the TV and his laptop. The TV was talking about football and Kelly loved football.

"Smart man," I thought to myself and went in the guest room to check emails and my Facebook account again. I groaned as I saw that I had over 100 requests from my gaming buddies. I clicked and clicked and repeated that over and over again as fast as the laptop would let me. My wrist was starting to tingle with only 10 to go, so I shook my arm out a bit and finished the last of them off just as I heard Kelly at the front door. I quickly signed out of everything, closed the laptop and went out to the living room again.

"Hello handsome!" she called to me as I came around the corner. She was setting down what appeared to be a moderately sized box of beer. As she pulled the different items out, however, it was clear that the box was just that, a box.

Charlie noticed the growing pile of things she was placing on the dinette table and asked, "what all have you got there sweetie?"

I sat down in the living room with Charlie as we watched her. She was beautiful as usual, in a pale green sundress that showed off her legs very nicely, in my opinion. From the smile Charlie was wearing, he appreciated her dress too.

"I decided to stop at Harry's and pick up some seafood for tonight," she told us, continuing to unpack the box. "You guys can have your choice of crab legs and shrimp...but the oysters are all mine."

Charlie looked over to me, as her back was to us, and smiled big and gave a knowing wink. I was a little unsure about what he meant until she announced the wine we'd be having with this special meal.

"And tonight, I am picking the wine for dinner, Chuck," she emphasized to Charlie using the nickname he hated, probably to get a rise out of him. It did.

"Better watch it or you'll get a spanking," he warned her playfully.

"I'm counting on it," she said with a giggle as she held up the bottle of rose' for us to see. The label read, *Ménage a' Trois*. Then she spun around and set it on the table. "Can you boys get this open for me and set some plates and stuff while I go freshen up?" she asked us leaving to go to the master bath in Charlie's room.

We got up to open the wine and set the table. Charlie handed me some plates and I set them down as he whispered, "if you haven't guessed yet, she wants us all to have a threesome."

"Really?" I asked back, "Are you sure?"

"Oh, yes, she really gets off on them sometimes and since she's sleeping with both of us separately anyway, well..." his voice trailed off as he handed me a fistful of silverware.

"I've never done anything like that," I confessed to him, more than a little concerned about the prospect.

"Don't worry and just let her lead," he said, "and don't worry about the pangs of jealousy you might get, they are just pangs and they disappear quickly."

I looked a little puzzled at him, which he noticed, and said, "Like I said, we've done it a couple of times so I know the feeling."

"Okay," I whispered back, "I'll just roll with whatever happens." My mind swirled with strange thoughts of the three of us, trying to envision what might happen after dinner. My thoughts didn't help, however, as I already felt a bit of jealousy creeping over me just at the prospect of having to share Kelly in that way. I wasn't sure if I could go through with it or not, actually.

116

I set the silverware out and Charlie set the now open bottle of wine on the table. He got three wine glasses out of the cupboard and set them near the plates. He went over to put the box away and noticed it still had one item inside.

He picked it up and showed it to me saying, "She definitely wants to play." It was a can of Redi-Whip whipped cream, the kind that sprays out of a nozzle. We both chuckled and he set it on the kitchen counter.

"Shouldn't that go in the 'fridge?" I asked.

"No!" he whispered excitedly, "that stuff is cold as heck out of the refrigerator. We've got to let it warm up a bit."

"Ahh," I replied. "They had apparently done that before as well," I thought to myself. This was going to be some strange night, I could tell already. A strange mix of anticipation and anxiety, as well as morbid curiosity swept over my insides as we finished getting the table ready.

Kelly came back into the room beaming with a glowing energy and bright smile.

"All right boys, let's eat," she said and sat down at the middle chair that was set for her. We all held hands again and said grace, which was still new for me but was rapidly becoming a custom I enjoyed, considering everything Charlie and I talked about the last few days.

Then we dove in to the meal. She started preparing her oysters. She must have managed to get the cook at Harry's seafood restaurant to crack them open for her, so she was having an easy time of it. Charlie split the crab legs and shrimp with me and poured us all glasses of wine.

"Mmm," Kelly said sensually as she swallowed the first oyster. The look on her face was almost sexual.

"You sure do like your oysters," I teased at her as she put the second one in her mouth.

"You have no idea," Charlie answered for her, chuckling at the whole scene.

"He will in a little while," she taunted back at us both, turning to wink at me to emphasize the point. It was not lost on me. I jumped slightly when I felt her hand squeeze the top of my thigh under the table, to which she giggled naughtily.

We all ate well and slow, having fun with the tastes and sensations of the food and wine and playing silent mind games with each other across the table as we chewed the food and licked various sauces from our fingers. The buildup was nearly maddening as she had both Charlie and I well worked up by the time the meal was done.

Kelly finished her wine and oysters and held her glass up so Charlie could refill it and he did. She got up from the table as Charlie and I watched, still finishing the food on our plates as she went into the living room and muted the TV. Then she went to the stereo and fumbled through Charlie's unorganized piles of CD's looking for the right one. She found it and put it in the CD player, adjusting the volume as the music started.

The music played out of the speakers and we watched, no longer eating, as Kelly's body swayed to the music with her back to us. We watched as her sexy legs and back kept time with the music, nearly hypnotically.

Charlie leaned over and whispered to me, "Go over and dance with her while I clean up."

"Okay," I answered back, unable to take my eyes off of Kelly's swaying backside.

He touched my shoulder to wake me from the trance she had me in and I looked up at him.

"Go," he said again.

This time I got up from the table and walked over to where Kelly was dancing alone. I approached her from behind and wrapped my arms around her waist as I pulled her into me.

"Mmm," she said quietly, "I'm glad you're here."

I leaned in and kissed her neck and told her, "I am too."

She continued to grind her hips to the music as I placed soft kisses on her neck and listened to her moans of appreciation.

"Unzip me," she requested and I leaned back enough to find the zipper to her dress and started pulling it down. As I did the dress started pulling away from her body, slithering down to the floor as a piece of silk might do. Now she stood swaying in only her heels and bra and matching panties, green this time like her eyes. She suddenly turned around and wrapped her arms around my neck and kissed me passionately as she once again tore at the buttons of my shirt.

Thinking that I'd rather not lose another shirt this time, I reached down and quickly helped unbutton it for her. She pulled the shirt off of me just as Charlie came in to the room carrying the can of Redi-Whip.

"Forget something?" he asked, holding the can up.

"Ooh, thanks sweetie," Kelly exclaimed then took the can from him, telling him, "now get undressed."

Then she took the can and sprayed some cold whipped cream on my chest, which gave me chills. Charlie was right, that stuff was cold! I was glad he kept the can out of the refrigerator. Next, Kelly leaned down and licked the creamy substance off of me. The sensations of the cold cream and her warm tongue made me moan uncontrollably.

"This is fun!" she said, swiping the cream from her mouth with her finger then sucking on it sensually while looking into my eyes. She told me to get undressed as well.

Charlie and I were both wearing just our underwear and checked each other out, as guys do. We nodded at each other and turned our attention back to Kelly, who was taking off her bra and panties. She picked up the can again and sprayed some cream on her right breast and walked over to me.

"This one if for you," she said as I leaned down eagerly to clean up the cream with my mouth. She moaned deeply in appreciation as I cleaned the cream off of her.

She then pulled away and walked over to Charlie, repeating the process with her left breast and telling him, "and this one is for you."

I watched as he leaned down to clean her up and felt the first real 'pang of jealousy' that he had mentioned earlier. "Oh, I see now," I thought to myself, "it's instinct." Jealousy is funny, it stems from a sense of 'ownership' but she was not my girl or even Charlie's girl, I reminded myself, she was her own girl and she was doing what made her happy. I decided to stick with that thought and let things happen as she directed them.

They broke from the game they were playing and she pulled Charlie over to where I was standing near the futon.

"Pull it out," she told him and Charlie set about changing the futon from a couch shape to more of a bed shape as she turned and kissed me again. She broke the kiss and whispered, "Let's play for awhile."

With that, she sat down on the futon and leaned back expectantly. I lay down next to her as I watched her give Charlie the 'come here' motion with her finger. He came over and got on the futon on the other side of her. As I watched her lean over to kiss Charlie, the next 'pang' hit me, harder this time. Something about this situation just didn't feel 'right'. I chased the thought away in my head and leaned over to kiss her neck. I reached over to where the Redi-Whip can was and grabbed it. I shook the can a little then carefully sprayed a little on her back, causing her to jump slightly. I eagerly leaned in to clean up the cream, kissing her back and at the same time blocking Charlie from my view. That seemed to help with the jealousy a little.

"I am loving this!" she declared after a moment or two, then lay flat between us and patted the mattress on both sides next to her.

"Get those off and get over here," she instructed us, pointing to our underwear.

I peeled mine off; feeling very strange for us all to be naked together at the same time, then shrugged that feeling off too. This was Kelly's night to have fun; Charlie and I were just along for the ride. I lay down on the futon where she had indicated, completely naked in front of my friends now and clearly excited. Charlie was lying next to her on her left.

She leaned towards me and kissed me very sensually, then broke the kiss and leaned over to Charlie and kissed him. I tried to relax and just stared at the ceiling in near disbelief that any of this was actually happening.

The rest of the evening passed in a mix of sexual pleasures and battling the feelings of jealousy and guilt as we 'played' together. That's how she kept referring to it, anyway. We did everything that Kelly asked of us and for the most part, it was enjoyable but everything was tinged with a dark sense of the forbidden. Still, I stifled my objections and participated, reasoning that it was all for Kelly's sake and making her happy was my only concern. I fought back the dark feelings as best I could and kept my focus on her as my only priority.

By the time we were done playing and satisfying Kelly in every imaginable way, we all fell asleep on the futon together with Kelly in the middle and a half-empty can of Redi-Whip laying on the ground and an empty bottle of wine on the coffee table. At some point, Charlie had gotten a blanket out of the closet and threw it over all of us so we wouldn't get too cold during the night.

Of course, she was the first one to get up the next morning and was already showered, dressed and cleaning up the kitchen when I finally stirred. I got up and found my underwear and pants and put them on. Charlie was still laying there naked and sleeping. I went over to the kitchen where Kelly was.

"Good morning, lover," she told me as she saw me heading towards her. She came over and hugged me hard and kissed me.

"Thank you for last night," she said, "that was even better than my fantasy."

"I should be thanking you," I told her, "you are amazing." I tried to make it sound as if I had enjoyed last night as much as she did; but it was a bit of a lie. As much as I did enjoy being with her, the sense of 'wrongness' of what we'd done overshadowed the good feelings for me. It was nothing like our afternoon together the day before.

"I'm glad you think so," she smiled back and kissed me again.

We broke the kiss and she stepped back and said, "You look like you could use some more sleep."

"I do," I confirmed simply. I didn't say much on purpose, not wanting to say something that would upset her and eager to get to a bed where I was alone for awhile.

 "Go lie down in your room and get some rest sweetie," she told me then kissed me on my cheek and patted my behind as I turned to go to the bedroom. "I'll finish up here then I have to get to work."

I did as I was told and stumbled off to the guest bedroom and lay down on the sofa bed, grateful for the closed door that muffled the noises coming from the kitchen as she cleaned up the place. I fell back asleep after hearing the front door close as she left the apartment once again.

Proverbial nightmares...

I got back up after a couple of hours more sleep. I needed a shower and a toothbrush. Walking back and forth between the guest bedroom and bathroom, I could see that Charlie was up and working on his laptop. I went about the business of getting cleaned up and ready for the day. Once I was dressed and my accounts online were checked, I sighed and closed the lid to my laptop slowly.

"Time to ruin my day already?" I thought to myself as I went in to the living room and sat down across from Charlie.

"Good morning," I addressed him somewhat hesitantly.

"Good morning back at you," he replied. A quick scan around the apartment revealed he had cleaned up from the night before as well, including picking up the living room. There was literally no evidence at all of what had transpired last night, other than the surreal memories floating around in my mind.

We sat in silence for a few moments then I said, "I didn't know Kelly was so...wild."

He looked up and smiled, clearly talking about Kelly helped divert his mind from the other things that lurked there.

"You will learn," he said, chuckling at me. "So, do you have any questions?" he posed to me.

I thought long and hard about everything we had talked about prior, all very scary stuff. The subject was like a loose tooth, however. No matter how much it hurt, I wanted to keep playing with it.

"So God hates America?" I asked weakly, "I suppose that makes those Westboro people right."

"Oh, Hell no!" he exclaimed immediately. "What I am talking about and those crazies have absolutely nothing to do with each other. They are the most preposterous group I've ever heard about, protesting at soldier's funerals...they are ridiculous!"

Charlie was clearly heated up over that group.

"For one thing, they think we are being punished for fighting the wars in the Middle East," he started, "and if I am right, then that's one of the only things we are doing right, right now. Hell, the Islamic terrorists are the synagogue of Satan, for crying out loud. Plus, it's not those soldiers' or their families' faults; they were just following orders and gave their lives fighting the good fight, or so they thought."

I nodded in silent agreement as he spoke.

"For another, if they believe that seriously that we are in Armageddon, as I do, then they should realize that the Catholic Church is the 'one true church' and give up being Baptists. It is the many schisms of Christianity that have weakened the Christian nation as much as anything that have 'caused' the problems. The same goes for all of the Protestant versions of Christianity and even the Anglicans. Once the different churches started splitting off and teaching their differences of opinions, the differences have grown significantly and not everyone who calls themselves 'Christian' actually demonstrate a correct understanding of the true Church's stance on things. Because we don't have a coherent, single population of like-minded Christians around the world, it's harder to fight a religious war, which is what the Islamic terrorists are doing; and groups like the Westboro fools are just as much a part of the problem as the fornicators and whoremongers, in my opinion."

"When you put it that way, it makes sense," I responded, "the different brands of faith make Christianity weaker, not stronger."

"Exactly," he agreed and went on, "remembering the mentions of the 'lady' in the Revelation story, let's talk about this country and its history. At first, it was just the 'gold rush of the Old World', the European countries claiming pieces of it from Canada to South America."

"Right," I interjected.

"After that, the parts that were the original USA were just properties owned by England, or the Anglicans and I mean that culturally and not as a religious label, who are favored by the Revelation story and Nostradamus. I think that has something to do with that strange passage in Genesis 6, actually. Anyway, there was no religious freedom in this country at first and it wasn't Christ's church that was here first. There was the Spanish settlement in St. Augustine but I'm talking about when the Pilgrims arrived and started the original thirteen colonies. Heck, Virginia, the first colony, made everyone who came there swear an oath to the Protestant church for the privilege. Maryland was a little more relaxed but you could say that the entire country was Christian at first, when the story is treating us nicely, even though made up of mostly non-Catholic faiths."

"True enough," I agreed, "the concept of religious freedom didn't come about until the Revolution."

Charlie nodded in agreement with me and went on, "Right, and if you believe that the Catholic Church is the 'one true church' which would appear to be the case looking backwards through time, then the problems in our country and the rest of the world go all the way back to Henry VIII, Luther, Calvin and Cromwell, who because of their actions splintered off thousands of Christians from the main church, thus taking away a tremendous amount of political power from the main church and making it more difficult to fight a religious war. Besides that, the formation of the Protestant, Baptist, Methodist, Lutheran and other schisms have incompletely or incorrectly taught their congregations about the religion; and, in addition, gave rise to everyone in the country questioning all of the Bible's messages since those offshoots started doing it first. Now we have a country full of so-called Christians who think just believing in Jesus is 'good enough' but the Bible and the Catholics teach that not everyone who says 'Lord, Lord' will get into Heaven. So, like I said, if you believe in the Bible then you have to believe all of it, including the Catholic Church's authority over the Christian religion."

"That's a pretty bold claim," I told him as I sat back in the chair and thought about it.

"Look at it this way," he sat forward as he continued, "from the very start for over 1,500 years there was only one Christian church and that was the Catholic Church. Then along comes Henry VIII who wants a divorce from his barren wife and asks for an annulment from the Church. Rightly so, because the marriage was legal from the Church's perspective, the Pope didn't grant him one. I mean, of all the disputes among the Christians the subject of divorce seems pretty easy to understand. 'Whoever divorces his wife and marries another commits adultery against her'…period. This is not a 'parable' or something given with a mixed message, it's quite clear. Anyway, after Henry, Mary becomes queen and the English church is restored by Rome in 1555; which coincidentally is the year Nostradamus published his book."

"Whoa, that's a heck of a coincidence!" I blurted out.

"Yes it is and I don't believe in coincidences. If everything has a meaning then just that fact should be telling us something. Of course, after that Elizabeth takes over and in 1558, the English church splits again and eventually becomes even more tainted by the Protestant Reformation by the time they start settling our country. Now, thanks to our great 'inventiveness' there are over 30,000 different versions, or denominations, of Christian churches out there; everything from the Amish to Christian Scientists and I'd say that since there are so many different variations it sort of proves by default that the original Church is the only one sticking to the original teachings and the rest just prove that once you take away the authority, you can't stop individual interpretation from changing the messages. I mean, 'Christian Science'…give me a break!"

"Okay," I said hesitantly, following along but unsure of where he was going with his thoughts.

"So, back to the point, the Founding Fathers write the Declaration and Constitution and a great nation was 'born'. That coincides with the imagery of the woman being 'with child' in her first mention of the Revelation story. But they went with Freedom of Religion and it was okay enough for awhile, since that meant a question of which Christian church to go to for most people. We fought alongside the English against the second 'beast' that was Hitler, then after World War II things turned south for us. The hippies, New Age movements, the rise of secularism and paganism and the free expression of sex without a believable, solid moral code or belief system to accompany it have been wearing our moral fabric down. We built huge memorials to our Presidents and war heroes but we won't do the same for God as a nation for fear of offending someone, even though the Founding Fathers intended us to be 'One nation under God'; and I can guarantee you they didn't mean Shiva or Allah."

"Well, that's certainly true," I agreed with his last comment, "everything in the Declaration and Constitution points to a 'Creator' and 'God' in the wordings. The documents all have a very Christian tone to them."

"Exactly but look how far we've strayed from that vision today. People are protesting the National Day of Prayer, religious holidays, crosses and other Christian imagery in government buildings and nearly all public displays of religion under the guise of 'political correctness'. Plus, the constant battles by the Freedom From Religion groups and others has us taking prayer out of schools and from all public life. Worse yet, groups like Planned Parenthood are moving into those same schools that prayer and God are being forced out of and teaching kids from middle school to college that masturbation, fornication, contraception and abortion are all 'good things' when the truth is the Church and the Bible teach the exact opposite. The problems extend to every aspect of our society. We've become so accustomed to 'me, me, me' and 'instant gratification' it is not funny. In fact, look at who the most famous, most profitable company in the world is right now," he explained.

"So you think God's mad at us because of Apple?" I asked.

"Well, there's no way of knowing if that's a part of it or not," he explained, "what I do know is that whoever had the visions in the Revelation story certainly believed that our country will be greatly punished for its abuses; but that is a judgment call, so to speak. If that person had visions of 9/11 and the other disasters, for example, and they were mixed in with flashes of what goes on in New Orleans and Las Vegas and abortion clinics, I could see where that would be the message they got. As for the Apple logo having the bite out of it, it is like putting the notion of original sin right in God's face; and not as something that we did wrong but something we are celebrating. But that doesn't explain other things, like why not India? If the Catholics are right and everyone else is wrong, why not smite the Hindus or the Buddhists?"

"Good question," I replied. After giving it some thought I added, "Maybe because they weren't supposed to get the message but we were. Maybe because of all we have in this country and for all of our political and cultural influence, we could have set a better example for the rest of the world. Or maybe it's like you said before, we are the only country who really could stop the Russians, so for all of this to play out we have to be taken out."

"Hmm," he pondered my suggestion, "I don't like the sound of that."

"What do you know," I thought to myself, "I made him feel uncomfortable for a change."

He shook his head as if to get the thought I had put there out of it and went on, "But it's a matter of perspective and perception in my opinion. I mean, who professes to know the mind of God? Certainly from St John's, or whoever's, perspective it would seem that we are being punished but consider this, what if the story is the story and it has been since what we consider the 'dawn of time'. I mean, the stars and planets and constellations and everything were well in-place long before there even were any humans; so maybe there was nothing we could do to stop it. Maybe that's just the way it is no matter what we do. Maybe we are a failed experiment, maybe we are a 'bad batch' or maybe, just maybe, we lived and will die exactly as we were supposed to."

I thought about that for a few moments, adding simply, "Maybe." I wasn't feeling too positive about Charlie's conviction that 'it is what it is'. Actually, the more we talked the more I wanted to go to church.

"Remember when I said that Nostradamus refers to us as 'Romans'?" he asked me.

"Yes, I remember you saying that," I answered.

"Take a look at Century two, quatrain number 8 and the footnote," he said, pushing the book over to me again. I read it.

Quatrain number II-8 reads, in English:

"Temples consecrated in the original Roman manner,
They will reject the excess foundations,
Taking their first and humane laws,
Chasing, though not entirely, the cult of saints."

I saw that the word 'excess' was footnoted and read that it could also mean fat, rude, disorderly, or unmannerly. I looked up at him, waiting for his explanation.

"That quatrain, and specifically line 1, is describing America, unlike Mr. Leoni's explanation offered in the back of the book which tries for a more literal meaning of the word 'temples'. Look at Washington D.C., nearly all of the Architecture there is Greco-Roman inspired, from the government buildings to the monuments, or 'temples' if you like. Look at the Lincoln or Jefferson memorials, those could easily be classified as 'temples' considering how most Americans idolize the early Presidents."

"Okay, I'm following you so far," I told him.

"Now, given the translation issue with the word 'excess' in line 2, we have to consider lines 2 and 3 together. Individually they are too vague to nail down but together they are describing how our founding fathers established our laws as laws of man, rather than God's laws, or the laws of the Catholic Church, which were much more extensive and restrictive from a civil rights perspective. Our laws are actually based on Masonic law more than anything."

"Well, that's true," I answered.

"The reference to 'first and humane' refers, I believe, to the Constitution and original Bill of Rights, which we still argue and bicker about to this day," he continued. "The last line is key to understanding that this quatrain is about us. We have always made it a point of not listening to the Vatican about things like wars, abortions, birth control, etc. Plus, in offering the people 'freedom of religion', which unfortunately now also includes Satanism, Paganism and the New Age stuff too, we've allowed all sorts of immoral ideas and activities as 'protected freedoms'. In fact, the Protestant nature of our country had so many people worried about the Vatican having any control at all since it was formed, that we've only ever had one Catholic President; and he was killed for it."

I looked at him thinking for a moment when he added, "Kennedy."

"Oh, yeah," I said, remembering that he was indeed Catholic.

"Getting back to the Revelation story, however, there are other sources for the end of times and Armageddon too, like in the book of Daniel that do not include the same accusations. Read Daniel 7," he said, sliding the New American Bible over to me.

I opened it and sure enough, it was talking about the four beasts again. I recognized that some of the imagery was the same, although they appeared in a different order with slightly different descriptions and Daniel had not included any reference to 'the lady' or the other terrible events in the Revelation story.

"I see what you mean," I said looking up.

"Want to see something funny?" he asked me. I could not imagine what in this conversation he could find that was 'funny'.

"Take a look at Daniel 4," he said, "start with verse 26 and read to verse 30."

I read the passages describing the boastfulness of King Nebuchadnezzar and how he was to be cast out from men and dwell with wild beast, eat grass and basically live like an animal for some time.

"Okay, notice the reference to the number seven again?" he asked.

"Yes," I answered.

He continued, "Now in the book of Daniel there are a lot of his predictions that were written and immediately explained as having happened at the time but think about this alternative translation: that in the seventh millennium the ruler of Bagdad, which was part of Babylon at the time, will be driven from men and found rag-tag in the fields like the beasts."

"You don't mean…" I started to say.

"Yep," he interrupted me, laughing, "Saddam Hussein. Remember the photographs from when we found him, buried in the sand, hiding out in the fields with his face and hair all raggedy. It fits this description perfectly."

I set the book back down on the table and thought. That was kind of funny in a chill-down-the-spine way. At least it was something bad happening to someone who deserved it.

"Want to see something even funnier?" he asked again.

"Sure," I replied, after all there was no stopping him when he was rolling.

"Check out Century eight, number 14," he directed.

I flipped the pages of the Nostradamus book and read the passage.

Quatrain number VIII-14 reads, in English:

> "The great credit, the abundance of gold and silver,
> Will cause honor to be blinded by lust,
> Known will be the offense of the adulterer,
> Which will occur to his great dishonor."

"Sound like anyone you know?" he asked.

I looked at the lines and considered their meaning and took a guess, "Bill Clinton?"

"You got it!" he stood up and exclaimed, "During Clinton's presidency, our country actually had a balanced budget...no deficit, we had very low unemployment and we were probably at our strongest financially and economically to fit the description for line 1. Lines 2 and 3 explain themselves from what we know about 'Slick Willy' and line 4 basically describe the look on his face in every interview since he was caught when he's asked about it."

He saw that I was thinking and continued to talk as I sat back down in the chair to listen.

"This is how I think this Armageddon thing works: First, Russia has been waiting for China to take over the world economy, which it pretty much has very recently with the global recession. There are already talks about moving the world economy off of the US Dollar, possibly to the Yen, and their spending is the only thing keeping the global economy going right now."

"True enough," I agreed.

"Take another look at Revelation chapter 13," he said.

I picked up the Bible and read as he spoke, "The lines about the first, greater beast indicates that they will be fueled by a 'dragon'. Using the conventional national imagery that would be the Russian, or Soviets or whatever they will call themselves, being supported by not only the threat of the Chinese joining the war but also their economy. If Russia managed to lock China into a deal that the two of them would only trade with other communist nations, they'd have the backing they'd need to pull it off. Not to mention with China controlling the value of the world's currency, that would serve well enough to 'fuel the fire' so to speak."

"Hmm," I mumbled in uneasy agreement.

"Also, we Americans have just gone fully digital and most of us are running around with iPads and cell phones and laptops and a lot of people only have satellite TV and no traditional home phones."

"Also true," I again agreed uneasily.

"Okay, so here's the scenario: Russia and China make their agreement and either take us completely by surprise with a nighttime attack during some distraction like Christmas or the Super Bowl; or issue a global threat and we refuse to bow down to them. I personally favor the former over the latter, since we are the one country that could take them down if we had advance warning. I figure a sneak attack and then they release a global threat to Europe and the rest of the world; but either way it fits. With the US out of the way and unable to help, England, France, Germany and the rest would either all have to wage war together or bow down to the trade demands of the Soviets and the Chinese, giving them power over all nations and tongues. The passage that talks about making war with the holy ones and overcoming them describes that Europe might fight back at first but may quickly surrender to the extreme threat of nuclear attack and economic meltdown; and also that religions will be suppressed as they were before in the first Soviet empire."

My heart pounded and my ears rang as I read verses 1-8 while he spoke.

"That scenario fulfills that prophecy exactly," he said and I couldn't disagree.

I set the Bible down nervously and told him, "Wow, that's serious business."

You bet," he continued, "and since we've all gone high tech, when the electromagnetic pulse from that initial attack takes place, every cell phone, computer, digital TV, iPod, iPad, and everything else with a computer chip in it, like cars, are all going to go dead for hundreds of miles around the blast zones. Let's say they launch 4 missiles, two traditional ones at military and commercial communications satellites, two nuclear missiles at New York City and Washington. The satellites go down just before the other nukes hit, and then the pulses occur; and no one in the country is going to know what's going on except for the few people with old phones and analog TV. The military's response will be slow and sluggish due to communications problems and the search for 'who is in charge'. When the news finally hits the people, there will be a panic to leave all of the bigger cities and to get away from the blast clouds and radiation fields."

"Probably so," I answered back. Considering the scene he was building in my mind, it was typical human behavior in panic situations like the one he was describing to me.

"Now look at Century ten, quatrain number 65," he told me.

I reached down for the Nostradamus book and again flipped through the pages and found the verses.

Quatrain number X-65 reads, in English:

> "O vast Rome, thy ruin approaches,
> Not of thy walls, of thy blood and substance:
> The one harsh in letters will make a very horrible notch,
> Pointed steel driven into all up to the hilt."

He spoke as I read, "Line 1 means the US, figuratively of course, and possibly Rome, Italy too from a literal sense if you factor in the Fatima visions. This is a warning of the attacks to come. Line 2 indicates that the bombs that are coming aren't going to physically destroy everything in the country but would kill many people and render our 'substance' ruined, such as with the aftermath of a nuclear attack leaving the lands unlivable and un-farmable. The American real estate and agricultural markets form much of the wealth of our country and, indeed, much of the world is invested heavily in our lands. Line 3 describes the Russian or Soviet leader that launches the attack. Nostradamus makes many mentions of 'harsh in letters' and the 'great one'; indicating the larger 'beast' from the Revelation story. The 'horrible notch' refers both to the blast zone itself and, I believe, a tongue-in-cheek reference to a 'notch in his belt'. Line 4 is vaguely describing the nuclear missile piercing the ground well past its length, again providing a description of a nuclear missile strike."

"Now go to Century ten, number 74," he instructed and I reluctantly complied.

Quatrain number X-74 reads, in English:

"The year of the great seventh number accomplished,
It will appear at the time of the games of slaughter:
Not far from the great millennial age,
When the buried will go out from their tombs."

I looked up at him, waiting for the translation.

"Okay, we've already been over the fact that this all happens in the seventh millennium and that we are in the seventh millennium."

"Right, I remember that conversation from the other day," I answered.

"So this has to be after 2001 for line 1," he explained, "in line 2, I believe 'it' is the nuclear strike and I believe the 'games of slaughter' indicate our sport of football, which is seriously like a modern, more strategic version of the Roman games and gladiators. Now, I will allow for the option that the 'it' could also mean the earthquake that turns the Sun black and the Moon red, as it is supposed to be the sign that this horror is all God's work. That's the only two 'it's' I believe this quatrain to be referring to. The Mayans indicated 2012 as a significant year when some great 'truth' will be discovered, and Nostradamus indicates the great ones will be awoken at the proper time in that other quatrain I showed you. So, honestly, it could happen at any time."

My eyes started opening wide in horror as he spoke. Charlie was making a compelling argument.

"That being said, I honestly believe that the attack will come during a Super Bowl or during playoff season. Line 3 once again refers to the entry in the seventh millennium and that the attacks aren't that far after the year 2001, so let's just say I've been scared out of my mind for the last few football seasons."

"I'll bet," I said as a cold chill moved through my mind and body.

"Line 4," he continued, "can be easily explained. The blast will blow everything out of the ground for miles in New York. Also, at the other end of that fault line that connects them to New Orleans, which is technically below sea level, they 'bury' their dead above ground in 'tombs' which will most certainly give up their dead when the big earthquake hits them."

"Whoa!" I responded. Everything certainly did seem to make sense and the whole scene was horrific if he was right. I caught myself praying he was not. "Damn," I exhaled as I agreed with him, sadly. He did appear to be on to something. "What about man not supposed to know the times of things?"

"Well," he answered, "I can't say exactly when everything will go down but I suspect it any time between now and 2021, given the math that Nostradamus has done for us. That means we still do not know exactly the time or date, however, both Nostradamus and the Revelation story refer to a moment that man finally figures out that it is Armageddon and the Lord himself is smiting the Earth. The 'time for the removal of ignorance' is how Nostradamus referred to it in the Preface and he has a quatrain about it too."

"So, what do we do now?" I asked.

"We wait and we watch and we worry," he answered, turning on the TV to watch the sports channels.

Kelly didn't come over that night so we heated up the leftover pizza from a few nights earlier and sat in mostly silence as we watched the talking heads talking about the various teams and how they might fare during their seasons.

To make a final point, he leaned over toward me and said, "Even our sports, right? We as a country don't respect soccer as much as our own brand of football. The NFL is even playing games in other countries now, just like the Roman games that traveled all over its empire; and Euro-Disney and Coca Cola and Marlboro and McDonald's…they are in nearly every country in the world. It's too bad, really. But then again, as I said before, this is the story…the script if you prefer…all of the time, no matter whose religion or mythology you look into. Eight millennia are all we get. Again, the question that really bothers me is why not India and the Hindus?"

"Well, maybe because they made a choice," I theorized back to him in response, "maybe we are being made an example of in the Bible's story, not because we allow for freedom of religion but because we've allowed our so-called freedoms to erode our moral responsibility. Maybe it's because we choose to be morally ambiguous when we should have chosen a side. Or because we should have been more generous with the very same thing that draws people to our country from other places… the lavish wealth of our resources. Maybe because everyone in the world looks to the US for a good example and we failed to provide one. Or maybe they get destroyed too but nobody cares."

"Hmm," he replied, "but still, did we have any other choice? The way the story plays out, it only makes sense in retrospect, so how could we predict we'd have an impact like this?" he cocked his head, adding, "Hmm…another Eminem reference, that's weird."

"No kidding," I said back, "you've got him on the brain. And like you said earlier, a lot of cultures have pieces to the end-of-times puzzle; it's just that none of them seem as 'judgmental' as the Bible's versions." I found myself making quote marks in the air like he did.

"Hmm," he mumbled back with a concerned look on his face.

We ate pizza, drank beer and went back to watching sports, occasionally making a comment about this player or that team; but nothing more of consequence. That night when I went to bed, I took the small Bible from the coffee table with me. I read some passages randomly, and then held it tightly as I prayed myself to sleep.

Doubting Thomas...

The next couple of days seemed to fly by in a repetitive cycle of waking, cleaning up, eating, talking about the end of the world until it hurt; then either having dinner and lighter conversation with Kelly or watching a mindless program on TV. Every day we delved further and further into the possibilities that Charlie was describing for the events to come, very soon according to him.

Oddly, the further we got into it, the less we drank and smoked. Neither of us said anything about it out loud but I know, for my own sake, I was getting a little worried about those kinds of things. Still, the conversation kept going deeper into the details of the story.

"Here, look at this," he'd say and I would look at the part of whichever book he was talking about at the time. This time it was a quatrain from Nostradamus' book.

Quatrain number VII-33 reads, in English:

"Through guile the realm stripped of its forces,
The fleet blockaded, passages for the spy:
Two feigned friends will come to rally,
Hatred long dormant to awaken."

I looked up and over at Charlie for his explanation, growing more weary and hesitant to listen to him.

"Assuming I am right about the US and Russia being the two 'beasts' or superpowers that start the Armageddon war and that this is coming soon, let's take a look at the world right now. We have massive national and global recession and meanwhile, we are wasting billions of dollars a month fighting a useless, un-winnable war in the Middle East…it's a distraction. Russia is our 'ally' right now in so much as they are waiting for our economy to go so far south that we lose our global political power base. So, for line 1, we are going to basically go bankrupt while we waste our time with the 'synagogue of Satan' and our military is spread out far too thin for what is coming to protect the country."

"Okay, fair enough," I said, following along.

"Line 2 tells us that something involving the Navy, or both Navies for that matter, occurs…some sort of blockade that allows for the escape or 'safe passage' of a spy that one or the other side wants. This hasn't happened yet but watch the news for it because this is the fuse being lit," he said.

"I will start paying more attention," I said through the nervous chill sweeping across me.

"Lines 3 and 4 are very easy, assuming I have the story right," he went on, "combined with those other predictions, America and Russia are the 'feigned friends', due to the deceit of Putin and our supposed cooperation in the War on Terror, which is just giving Russia a lot of intelligence on how we operate by 'helping' us fight the terrorists. Apparently, due to this spy controversy and a Naval blockade, the old hatred between the US and Russia is going to be re-kindled."

"I could certainly see that," I told him, "the Russians and the US have been enemies since we rose to power. Even in the movies and television shows, Hollywood seems to be playing this theme out with all sorts of stories about the pending war between our two countries."

"Exactly," he agreed, "you can't really put any other two countries in this prediction, or the whole story for that matter, at this point in time except for Russia, or the Soviets or whatever they become, and our country."

Another time he said, "Now take a look at this," and it was another Nostradamus prediction.

Quatrain number II-30 reads, in English:

"One who the infernal gods of Hannibal
Will cause to be reborn, terror of mankind
Never more horror nor worse of days
In the past than will come to the Romans through Babel."

Again, I sat back after reading it and waited for the gloomy explanation.

"Okay," he started, "this is one of the more vague predictions by Nostradamus in as much as it is not giving a lot of detail; and it has little meaning unless you know the story as we do. The entire quatrain is basically identifying the larger 'beast' or empire that will be attacking another nation. Again, I maintain that Americans are the 'Romans' as Nostradamus calls us, and that this again refers to Russia or the Soviets as the enemy that attacks us viciously and with nuclear weapons. Clearly, in all of the disastrous predictions he made, Nostradamus is making this 'terror of mankind' out as a worse terror than Hitler or anyone else in history; and is described as bringing our country more horror than we've ever known, which matches the result of an all-out nuclear strike."

"Interesting," I interjected, "it does seem pretty vague though."

"On the surface, yes," he explained further, "but not on closer examination, given what we've talked about before and moving forward with the working assumptions I started with. America is the new Rome to Nostradamus and if I'm right about 9/11 and the Twin Towers marking that city as 'new Babel' for this story, then it becomes much clearer for line 4. Whether terrorists nuke the city or Russian submarines do the job, the source of the weapons will be found to be from Russia. With America's predictable response to being attacked in mind, if we find out that the Russians are ultimately responsible, we will respond in kind and total nuclear annihilation is possible. Now, the Revelation story talks about the third beast, the greater of the two and more horrible, it mentions that the 'beast' speaks great blasphemies; and this prediction may be an indication that Putin or whoever it is will be spreading great blasphemes. In light of the Fatima visions, we are told that Russia will be used to punish the world, annihilate nations and spread atheism. A much simpler explanation of Hannibal overcoming actual Rome in ancient times as a figurative reference to the new conqueror of the 'new Rome' and 'new Babel' could be used to justify line 1."

"That would make sense," I said, again the sickening feeling overcoming me once again.

Another time I asked him, "So what's this about the moon being knocked out?"

"Oh, yeah," he said, "check this out."

He got the Nostradamus book out and opened it for me, pointing to a spot on the page. I read the quatrain.

Quatrain number I-48 reads, in English:

> "Twenty years of the reign of the Moon passed,
> Seven thousand years another will hold its monarchy;
> When the sun will take its tired days
> Then is accomplished and finished my prophecy."

"Okay," I said, "this seems pretty specific."

"That's the beauty of it," Charlie exclaimed, "because it is so specific, people constantly argue about when the starting point is; but if you've gotten this far into it, it's actually kind of simple. Of course, he's changed tense on us again, putting the 'present' not at the time of his writing but 20 after Creation, telling us the moon will reign 7,020 years total. The rest of it, mentioning the sun's demise and his prophesy being done takes us all the way to the end of the story of mankind. Interestingly enough, the part of the Revelation story talking about the sun and moon and stars being smitten happens early on in chapter 8, verse 12."

I got up and went over to the big Bible and thumbed through the pages to read the passage and a few others before and after it.

"Whoa," I said as I walked back, "so when does that happen?"

"Well, doing to the math, the moon lasts 7,020 years according to Nostradamus so the real question is the starting point. I might argue the Egyptian 4236 BC as 'year 1' but I'm not so sure. One could also argue Velikovsky's estimate that the moon actually came into our orbit in 3117 BC but again, I don't agree. Nostradamus, as a converted Catholic-Jew was well aware of the prophecies of both the Old and New Testaments and I could argue that he would have used the Judeo-Christian 3761 BC as their traditional starting point, which makes the year for this event around 3259 AD. However, if you read the Preface to the quatrains, as most people don't, you'll see that he actually calculates out his own year for the year of Creation at 4173 BC, which makes this event happening around 2847 AD."

"At least we'll be long gone by then," I quipped.

"Not exactly," Charlie cautioned waving his finger at me, "according to the Revelation story those who are saved are in the new city with the Lord for 1,000 years on Earth, while outside the city rages sin and war and famine; but the story says that death itself is thrown out so it may very well be our generation who suffers through this lengthy time period...unless you are in the Book of Life, of course. That explanation notwithstanding, one thing you have to keep in mind is that the Revelation story does not exactly occur in a linear timeline; and Nostradamus purposefully jumbled his predictions around so that it would be very difficult to put the events in a concrete timeline prior to them happening. Some of this is just guesswork until it happens."

"Of course," I managed a weak reply, thinking about the Book of Life seriously for the first time in my life.

Lake of fire...

It was Friday the 10th and Charlie and I had gone through a ton of information, theories and translations by this point. He had pretty much mapped out how the Great War will begin and who it involved and what some of the responses were going to be. I was curious to know what he thought about one more thing, however.

"So, what do you make of the lake of fire?" I asked.

"Oh, wow!" he exclaimed as his face lit up in excitement, "I'm glad you asked that. It's the coolest part of the whole story."

He stood up and paced behind the futon while he spoke, "assuming everything else in the story takes place as told and given the visual imagery of the Bible combined with the predictions by Nostradamus, I am guessing a black hole enters our galaxy close enough to start eating our solar system."

"How is that cool?" I quizzed him, wondering.

"Okay, follow me here. The image of a lake of fire could be the Earth going completely volcanic, which would certainly devour everything left on the planet in flames, however it doesn't fit being able to swallow the moon, the planet and the stars."

"Okay, right," I agreed curious to find out why he was so excited about the question.

"The only thing in all of space that man has been searching for seven millennia now that is big and bad enough to swallow the sun, earth, moon and stars and everything that was once 'us' as an entire story, complete with every last bit of matter and energy that once existed as 'man' is a black hole. I think that's why NASA spends so much time and money studying them."

"Okay, I'm listening," I said, still waiting for the 'cool' part of our solar system being eaten by a black hole.

"Remember my theory on how Creation and Evolution could both be right?" he queried.

"Yes, I remember that," I answered.

"Okay, keeping in mind the references of 'Alpha and Omega' that are so prevalent in the story and my theory that this is the Genesis story playing out in reverse, then the end of our story means the beginning of another story of man to occur upon our demise. The Revelation story refers to a new earth under new stars even; and definitely implies that the cycle repeats."

"Yes, it does appear that way," I answered back, impatient for his answer.

"Okay, now in the Big Bang-plus-Evolution theories of science, they can explain how everything happened from the Big Bang to the formation of the earth fairly well, they just can't explain the 'who' or the 'why' behind the Big Bang, which is what the Genesis story is for. Then you get to the formation of life on earth. The Darwinian's can explain a lot of the 'how' man evolved into modern humans but again, not the 'why' or 'by who' we gained awareness. They also cannot explain successfully just what caused the original 'primordial ooze' containing the basic building blocks of life to form in to DNA and the first simple organisms in the first place. Something caused it, or someone, but right now the best they can give is 'some sort of radiation coming from somewhere'."

"That sounds about right," I agreed, "both theories provide a lot of evidence after the fact but neither can really explain the cause of it all."

"Exactly" he continued, "they likewise have a hard time explaining exactly what caused man to 'wake up' and become aware of himself and his surroundings as a being. Again, they theorize about drugs, cosmic radiation, and a host of other ideas. I think that they both tie in to what is eventually going to happen to our solar system."

"How so?" I asked.

"Well, for a long time science was aware of these black holes and could tell they were eating up stars and planets but had a hard time finding them because they absorb all light, making them invisible. When they are eating a star, though, NASA can see their outline because as the black hole drains off a star's energy, it moves in a counterclockwise oval, following the lines of gravity being emitted by the black hole. It creates a flaming hurricane effect visually."

"Like a sea of fire," I commented in, mentally visualizing what he was describing.

"Exactly," he agreed, "which would once again literally support the imagery in the visions and explain how the sun, moon, earth and everything else get swallowed up in it. Again, it's not saying God isn't making it happen, it's just the best observable phenomena in the universe to describe the 'how' it could actually happen."

"Okay," I answered back, "that explains the death of everything but I'm missing the part that is cool."

"Ahh, yes," he continued, "and this is all just theory, of course. I won't be around to see it, that's for sure. Only very recently, using different frequencies and color bands, have scientists discovered where the resultant energy from all the matter and energy being absorbed by these giant devourers of planets is going. Invisible to the naked eye, the only thing that seems capable of escaping the tremendous gravitational pull of these black holes is a very tight beam of X-Rays that shoots out of the apex of their energy bands and blasts out for trillions of light-years, if not more, to who knows where."

"Hmm," I mumbled, "so what does that mean?"

"Connect the 'who knows where' of the black hole eating our galaxy up with Alpha and Omega references in the Bible and the 'comes from somewhere' aspects of the Big Bang and Evolution theories. Maybe, just maybe, another story is ready to begin on another planet in a solar system far away from here; and maybe the design is that the new planet is ready and the X-Rays coming off of our black hole are the radiation that sparks the first life forms or is what spawns awareness in the next race of men? Wouldn't that be cool?"

I thought about it for a bit. "I suppose so," I told him after a few moments, still considering it. The idea was nearly poetic in that the chosen ones get to leave with God but that the rest of us, and everything else around us along with it, are neatly converted into pure energy and help spark a new race of humans somewhere else in the universe. It was a really 'grand design' when I thought about it.

"So, let me ask you another question," I started tentatively, as I did not want to upset him too much but was curious about something else that had been nagging at me.

"Okay, shoot," he answered back.

"Well," I began hesitantly, "You seem to have reconciled a lot of the arguments between science and the Bible and the other sources; and pretty much have figured out, at least for yourself, the meanings of a lot of what is in it. Not to mention your opinions about churches and denominations."

"Yes," he said quizzically as I paused to find the right words.

"How come you aren't Catholic yet?" I finally asked him directly.

"That's a good question," he pondered out loud, "I've been thinking about that more and more as we talk about it. I guess it just always goes back to the fact that the pieces of truth about the beginning and end of life on this planet can be found in so many places, who knows what to do?"

"Well, maybe," I theorized at him, "that the point is that the Christian story is the only story offering a way out. The others can all tell you the 'what' or 'when' as you say; but not the 'why' or 'by who', not even science. Maybe that's the point of the whole thing. Given all of the available choices, it is the only belief system that's offering a lifeline to the other side."

He thought about my comments with a worried look on his face for a few moments.

"You may just be right about that," he admitted, adding, "but then what about the people who know no better? What about the tribes of Africa that have never heard the Bible or were able to make the choice? And the kids in America, who are the products of their mis-informed parents; what if by honoring their mother and father they accept the mark of the beast unknowingly? That doesn't seem very fair."

"No, it does not," I agreed, "but then again, who said life was fair? That's not written anywhere in the book. Besides, there has to be a 'bad guy', right? It's like that one story about Heaven being like a wedding party and the king sees someone there not in wedding garb and tosses them out. Maybe this whole exercise in human futility is the painfully long process by which God chooses the very select few who get to come to his party."

Charlie thought about that for a time and then he said, "Well, if that's the case then I'm sure I'm not invited to the party."

Clearly I had disturbed him by introducing the idea that the moral consequences may indeed be valid, considering that the rest of the story, according to him, seemed to work out. We sat in silence for some time after that. I sat thinking of God and black holes and X-Rays…I wasn't sure what Charlie was thinking but I could tell by the look on his face that it wasn't pleasant.

Lamentations...

The next morning I awoke first and crept out of the sofa-bed so as not to disturb Kelly. She had come over to the apartment late the night before, after Charlie had gone to bed, and slept with me. I remembered the feelings of joy I had when I rolled over to find her crawling in to bed with me, even though it was so late and I barely was able to greet her with little more than a mumble and a kiss before falling back to sleep. She moved very little as I stood up and looked down at her sleeping form. She was so beautiful. I got my pants on and went to the bathroom to relieve myself. Coming back, I noticed that Charlie was not sitting in his usual spot on the futon in the living room but gave it little thought at the time.

"Hmm," I mumbled to myself, "I must be the first one up." I didn't give it much more thought and snuck back into bed with Kelly for a little extra sleep time since it was Saturday morning and all. I was barely able to drift back to a light sleep when Kelly started to stir. She woke up quickly; it must have been because of all of those years working as a single woman and business owner that made her jump up so readily when she awoke. She got out of bed, dressed and went out into the apartment as I sluggishly followed suit and put my clothes on.

"Have you seen Charlie?" she came back to ask as I finished putting my shirt on.

"Not when I was up earlier," I told her.

"I'm worried, he's not in his room," she told me frantically.

I went out to see what was happening with Charlie and searched the apartment for clues. In the kitchen was a small sticky note near the coffee pot indicating that he had gone out for cigarettes and that the coffee pot was ready to be started when we got up. I flicked the switch on the pot to get the coffee going and went to find Kelly. She came out of Charlie's bedroom and met me in the living room.

"He's not in the shower either," she said, still frantic.

I tried to reassure her, "Calm down, sweetie, he left a note and he went out for smokes and will probably be back any minute."

She calmed down a bit and went to sit down on the futon, while I went back into the kitchen to get our coffee cups ready. A strange silence settled in the apartment, without the noise of the TV or Charlie's conversation to fill the background. Then we heard the sirens.

"Oh my God!" Kelly shouted and rushed to the front door. I followed quickly behind her, my heart pounding as I broke into a cold sweat even before we started running across the parking lot to the road where the police cars were sitting with their flashing lights beckoning. We nearly got to the sidewalk before Kelly suddenly stopped and fell to her knees.

"Oh God no, not Charlie," she sobbed.

I looked past her to the street where the police cars were circled. Charlie was sprawled out on the highway, looking like a broken doll amidst a swath of scattered cigarette packs from the carton he had just purchased across the street minutes earlier. About 20 feet in front of him was an old pickup truck, light blue, with a "Remember 9/11" bumper sticker on it.

In an eerie daze, I walked past Kelly, who was on her knees crying uncontrollably. I walked towards the scene with the whole world in a fuzzy haze as the sight of Charlie's lifeless form was burned into my retinas. I was barely aware of the chaos around me as men and women from the police department and ambulance scrambled to get the area secured. I remember hearing the truck driver's name as a police officer questioned him when I walked by. George Oliver Dudley was the man's name. Tightness gripped my chest and fear chilled my spine as the name reverberated in my head and I thought about his initials.

Suddenly, a police officer stopped me.

"You can't go in there," he said, breaking me momentarily out of the nightmarish reverie I was in.

"Oh," I said, reacting to being suddenly pulled out of thought, "that's my friend."

"You can identify the victim?" the officer asked me.

I thought about those words for a moment or two.

"Sir?" he asked again, and again I was pulled back into reality.

"Oh, yes, sorry," I scrambled to get out. I told him Charlie's name, where he lived, who I was, and pointed out Kelly to him. He asked me if I knew any immediate family. I told him that Charlie had a mother in town and that her number was on his cell phone, which was still in the apartment.

"Have it ready when we stop by," he instructed me, "and take care of your girlfriend over there. She needs some reassurance right now."

I looked over at Kelly and then turned back to thank him but he was already gone. I ran back to Kelly and shook her out of her sobbing.

"We have to get back to the apartment and clean it up," I told her insistently. I brushed back her tears with my hands and made her look at me. "The cops are going to be there any minute and they are going to call Charlie's mom."

She looked at me and her face returned to resolve as she understood what I wasn't saying but knew needed taking care of all too well. She stood and we both started walking quickly back to the apartment, stifling back our grief as the frantic need to cleanse Charlie's apartment gripped us. Our walking quickly became trotting, which then turned into a full run as we neared the front door.

"Okay," I told her as we reached the door, "we've got to get all of the pot and porn and the creepy religious stuff out of here."

Nearly out of breath, she asked, "what do you want me to do?"

I looked over at the parking spaces and noticed an open spot in front of the apartment. I nodded towards it, saying, "Back your car in to that spot and I'll start packing things up."

She ran off towards her car, pulling her keys out of her pocket as she tried to keep step. I could hear her get inside as I turned to enter Charlie's apartment. It was just as we'd left it minutes earlier yet now everything was different. Charlie wasn't here to call the shots anymore and we needed to get busy before the police and his mother arrived. I started pulling the flip chart pages off of the wall and piled them on the coffee table. I could hear the squeals of Kelly's tires as she moved her Mustang into the open spot.

She rushed inside as I was piling another set of books, asking, "Okay, my car is parked...what now?"

I looked up at her in a near panic as I piled the tremendous amount of papers and books Charlie had amassed in his research.

"You grab the pot and the porn and lock it in your trunk, I'll get this religious stuff out of here and in to my car," I instructed her. Her eyebrow tweaked up as she heard me.

"Interesting choice," she sort of half-joked back at me, her eyebrow cocked in that funny way she had when she was confused or worried about something.

I answered back, more seriously, "you know where all of that stuff is, and I don't. I can grab this stuff because it's right out in the open and it's a bigger pile." I added, "And it's less illegal, so we need that other stuff out of here now."

She nodded back at me, her eyes glassing over with sadness at my curtness but I couldn't let myself be weak on her behalf. Charlie's and our own reputations were at stake. She stood, stuck for a minute or two, and then the strength came back to her eyes and chin. She nodded at me and quickly went in to Charlie's bedroom. I saw the box from the dinner she'd brought a few nights back and went over to get it. I brought it in to Charlie's room to her and told her to pack everything she could in to the box.

She looked up at me with tearful eyes and admitted, "This is so hard, and there are so many memories in here."

"I know, Kelly," I tried to reassure her, "but you know we have to do this and quickly. Leave all of the memories for the moment and let's get this place ready for Charlie's mom to look through."

"Okay," she said nodding, her resolve returning once again.

I went back to the living room and looked around. I had just about everything to do with Armageddon and Nostradamus and the rest piled up somewhat neatly. I went to the guest bedroom and found my car keys, then returned to the living room. I grabbed a small pile of printed out news articles and went out to my car. I unlocked it and opened the trunk. I wasn't right in front of the apartment but it was just a few spaces down from where Kelly was parked, so it wasn't that bad of a walk. I put the papers in the trunk and arranged everything else in there to be ready for mine and Charlie's stuff.

I left the back door and the trunk open, little fearing anyone wanting to steal any of the stuff I was putting in the car. Heck, they could have it if they wanted it…as long as it wasn't lying around for Charlie's mom to see. I got back in the apartment and went for another stack of stuff. Kelly heard me coming in and yelled out the bedroom door at me.

"I'm taking my stuff out of here too," she announced.

I stopped in my tracks and, leaning my head back to answer, and told her, "Go right ahead, that's probably a very good idea."

I picked up another stack of Charlie's research and headed back to my car. I repeated the trips several times, nearly filling my trunk with books and printouts and papers. I was back in the apartment for another pile when I saw Kelly standing in Charlie's bedroom doorway.

"I need your help," she told me, "I have my stuff in a suitcase and all of the 'bad stuff' is in the box…but it's heavy." Funny, she made the quote marks in the air with her fingers just like Charlie used to do.

"Sure thing," I told her and reached down to lift the box. I stopped, readjusted my hands and tried a second time.

"I see what you mean," I told her as I straightened up, "it is heavy."

"Let's go," she said and picked up the suitcase and walked past me to the door. I followed more slowly, carrying the box full of Charlie's vices behind her. It was a short walk, since her car was so close and I waited as she pulled her keys out and opened the trunk. She leaned over to push her stuff around to make room for our load. She moved out of the way and motioned for me to put the box in. I quickly took the opportunity and rushed forward to set the box down, which I did with a thud.

I stood back up and stepped back, holding my lower back as I straightened up.

"Ouch," I announced as I moved back out of her way. She shut the trunk and moved to the passenger side of the car to put the suitcase in.

I quickly moved to open the door for her and moved the front seat forward.

"Thanks," she said simply and held out the handle of the suitcase for me to take. I did and hefted the suitcase into the back seat of her car, moving the front seat back in place after I did.

I stood up again, wincing slightly at my stiffening back and answered, "I do what I can, when I can." I winked as I told her that, trying to lighten our mood a little now that the misdemeanors were safely packed away. Now all I had to do was take care of the blasphemies that remained in the apartment.

I went quickly back in to the apartment and Kelly followed. I did a quick survey and saw that there were only a few stacks left of Charlie's research. I turned to Kelly and grasped her arm.

"Please," I pleaded with her, "take these last stacks of stuff out to my car. I have to get my things packed too."

She nodded, taking orders and acting on them like a seasoned veteran. I guess her adrenaline was pumping by this point. She went to gather up the last of the books and papers as I went back to the guest room to gather my things. I packed frantically, shoving my clothes and personal effects into my luggage. I felt a bit like a thief leaving a crime scene but we had to do what needed to be done. With my suitcase and laptop packed. I went back to the living room where Kelly waited for me, still in shock over what was happening.

As I rounded the corner of the hallway, I could see her sitting on the futon, wringing her hands, her face contorted in guilt, grief and regret. She heard my lumbering with the luggage down the hallway and jumped up to help me carry it out, as if looking for something to do to keep from thinking about Charlie.

I let her take the laptop case from me and we went out to my car together with my things. At my request we put both bags in the backseat of my car, since the books and papers had taken over my trunk and the luggage was much more 'explainable' should any questions be asked.

I shut the doors and the trunk to my car and we both walked back to the apartment in silence. Autonomously, we walked back in and took our seats in the living room as if everything were 'normal'. We sat like that for a few minutes then Kelly started crying again. I got up and went over to sit with her on the futon and tried to comfort her. I put my arms around her and held her tightly as she cried. She held me back, tentatively at first and more tightly after she let her grief take over her emotions. I held her back and we cried together as we waited.

Eventually, we were startled out of our grief by a harsh knock on the door. Kelly jumped in my arms and I pulled away to get up. I reached a hand to her cheek to wipe away her tears and tried to reassure her. I went over to the door and looked through the peephole. Sure enough, it was a police officer. I sighed, anticipating the questions and pain that were coming, and then opened the door.

"Come on in, officer," I said as I swung the door open. It was a somber greeting, not cheerful or excited but merely depressed as was I.

"Thank you," the officer told me, walking past me into the living area. I followed closely behind to 'see what he saw' and to anticipate helping Kelly with the questions.

I sat with her on the futon as the officer quizzed us. He handed Charlie's wallet to her and told us they had all the information they needed, except how to contact his next of kin. Kelly got up, wiping her face of tears, and went to Charlie's room to get his cell phone. As we waited, the officer tried to chat with me, asking how I knew the deceased, as he put it, and why I was staying at his apartment. I answered simply and honestly enough, leaving out the parts about Armageddon and Nostradamus, naturally. He was asking about Kelly and Charlie when she came back in the room.

"I was just a very close friend of his from high school," she answered the question herself as she came back into the room behind the officer, who turned to watch her as she sat back down beside me on the futon.

She looked through Charlie's contact list on the phone and asked if the officer was ready. He indicated he was, with a pen and small notebook in hand, and she read off the name and telephone number of Charlie's mother.

"That's the only way I know of to get in touch with her," she added, "I haven't actually seen her and Charlie together in years."

"That's fine, miss," he said, "if we can't reach her with this number, we'll do a search for her. You said she lives in town?"

"She lives in Hillsborough County somewhere," Kelly told him, "but I couldn't tell you if she lives in Tampa, Carrollwood, Temple Terrace or Brandon for that matter."

"Don't worry, we'll work with the Sherriff's Department to track her down," he told her back matter-of-factly.

Kelly dug through her purse for a moment then pulled out some pieces of folded paper.

"I have his will and I am the executor," she informed the officer. She looked at me and said, "I got it out of his desk when I got his cell phone."

I nodded at her as the police officer reached over and took the papers and eyed them quickly.

"So it would appear," he said as he handed them back to her, "hold on to that, you're going to need it. You might want to get an attorney too."

"You are probably right," Kelly started to reply, her voice trailing off into deep thought.

"Is that all you need?" I asked the officer impatiently.

"I'll need your names and contact information too, just in case," he told us.

Kelly told him her name, address and home and cell phone numbers and he wrote frantically to keep up with her. Meanwhile, I reached back to get my wallet out. When she was done, I stood up and handed a business card over to the officer. When he was finished writing down Kelly's information, he looked at me and took the card.

"It's got my mailing address and my cell number, which is all I have while I'm in town," I informed him.

156

"And how long is that?" he asked back.

"As long as she needs me to be," I said looking over at Kelly, "and she can get in touch with me if I need to leave for work or something."

He looked at us quizzically for a second, then folded his notepad and put it and my card in his front shirt pocket.

"That's all for now," he said, "I will be contacting the mother soon. I'm sure she'll want to get in touch about the will and the apartment."

I stood as he turned to leave and walked with him to the front door. When we reached it, he put his hand on my arm to stop me from opening it and leaned over to speak closely to me, out of Kelly's earshot.

"I saw a small tray with a pipe on it under the futon your girlfriend is sitting on," he whispered, "now, I'm not going to give you any trouble over it, you're having a rough enough day today; but you may want to clean this place up before his mother gets here."

My face and ears burned with the embarrassment of being caught and by the anger over missing the one place we all knew to check for that stuff earlier. I stifled my usual smartass comment back and turned the handle on the door to open it.

"Will do officer, and thanks," I said with a real sigh of relief.

"No problem," he said back, "and try to keep yourself and your girlfriend out of trouble too."

"Will do," I said again and watched him walk out and away to his patrol car.

I went back to where Kelly was sitting and crying on the futon. I knelt down and found Charlie's special tray underneath with the remnants of his last joint and some papers lying on it. I quickly walked it all over to the trash can in the kitchen and threw it away angrily. I took a deep breath to calm myself back down and returned to where Kelly was sitting.

"Well, at least that's over," I tried to reassure her again.

She reached over and hugged me tightly and said, "Oh, John, what are we going to do?"

I hugged her back as she sobbed against my chest and thought for a bit. Slowly the realization started coming to me, overwhelming the grief and worry, that we needed to do what Charlie had advised. He had been right about his death being untimely and the name of the driver of that truck gave me a sickening feeling when I thought of his initials. Charlie had told me exactly what to do if this happened; and I was suddenly swept over with fear for our very souls.

I leaned back from Kelly and held her head in my hands and looked as deep into her eyes as I could, saying, "Kelly, I love you. I always have. Charlie knew it and I think you do too. He told me what to do if something happened to him that 'freaked me out' and this situation is completely doing that. Do you understand me so far?"

She nodded, clearly still in shock from Charlie's death and my words weren't comforting her, they were scaring her.

"Did Charlie ever talk to you about the stuff he was telling me?" I asked her urgently.

"A little of the Nostradamus stuff but I stopped listening when he started talking about the Bible," she confided, "I don't think anyone has ever gone as far in the conversation with Charlie as you have."

"Okay," I continued looking at her deeply as I spoke, "I agree with a lot of what Charlie told me except for one thing. He tried pulling the predictions out of the prophecies and ignoring the messages about morality but I don't think we can do that. I honestly believe that everything he talked about is going to happen someday and I believe the religious and moral parts of the story as well. I believe in God and that we have souls and in Heaven and Hell and that we need to do something about it."

"Meaning…?" she left the question open for me to continue.

"I know this will sound crazy but Charlie and I talked a lot about what to do if anything happened to him," I started.

"Like us getting married, yeah…he mentioned that once or twice," she interrupted me. "I never thought it about it seriously, though."

I continued, "It's more than that, we need to get our shit together. You and I both. Charlie told me to make an 'honest woman' out of you and start going to church and a bunch of other crazy stuff that I never really expected to do but now that he's dead, I am afraid we may not even have the time to do everything he said."

"Like what?" she asked earnestly, looking as scared as I was at this point.

I told her about selling her business and our homes, buying gold and getting a boat...or even leaving the country completely and finding some place to hide. I told her about selling off nearly everything we owned, including Charlie's stuff, and making ourselves as 'portable' as we could get in case we needed to escape the nuclear holocaust and move to Europe somewhere. I told her about trying to survive the coming events as best we could; and I told her that we needed desperately to change our ways and start really, really trying to live properly in the Christian faith.

"I already am a Christian, I'm a Methodist and I go to church sometimes," she started to say, defending herself.

"No, that's not what I mean," I explained to her as I knelt down and gripped her shoulders in my hands, "I mean, if you believe the story as I do, you have to believe all of it. Including that the Catholic Church is the one true church and we need to join it; and we need to start living our lives better for the right reasons for a change. We have to live right and pray...pray for ourselves and for Charlie and for everyone we care about. No more of this screwing around."

She sat back to think about what I just told her. She was clearly overwhelmed with everything that was happening. I relaxed my grip on her sat next to her on the futon as she thought over what I said to her. We sat like that for some time, and then she turned to me and looked me deep in my eyes.

"Do you really love me? All of me, my past and present?" she asked me. I guess she was doing some quick soul-searching and confided in me, "I've done some pretty bad things you know, with Charlie and other guys and there was even this one time at a party where..." Her voice trailed off into silence and I could tell that she didn't want to share that last part with me; and then she looked down at the floor as if expecting a bad answer.

I lifted her head back up gently to look her in the eyes again and spoke from the depths of my heart, "I love you dearly. I always have and I always will, no matter what your past is filled with. You make my heart feel brighter and you melt my anger. If we really are nearing our final days, I would love to spend them with you, Kelly."

She smiled brightly through her tears at what I told her, then frowned again as I went on, "but even more importantly I want to spend eternity together with you. I want us to try to get out of Hell and at least into Purgatory and Heaven if possible. I want to be your husband not just your lover, and not just for tax purposes. I want us to be able to make love without shame or guilt and if we have the time, to confess our sins and try to beg God for forgiveness for both of our pasts. Believe me, I know we'll never be 'saints' but we can at least try to save our souls and make peace with God before the world goes to Hell in a hand basket."

She sat thinking hard again as I released her from my hands and sat back to wait for her response. She internalized for some time as I waited and watched her face go through the entire spectrum of human emotions.

"Okay, I'm still listening," she said looking up, "and I believe that you believe these things very strongly. It may take some time for it all to sink in for me but...I'm listening."

Inside my head, I actually yelled, "Thank God!" and I hugged her tightly. Then she was all back to business.

"Now, let's get the stuff we are really going to need," she announced, standing up as she did so.

"And what would that be," I said, marveling at how she could just turn like a switch on me at times.

"Bank account statements, copies of bills, life insurance records...that kind of stuff," she explained as she walked towards Charlie's room abruptly, "after all I am the executor and if we need to sell this stuff off, I need to know what the bills are and what kind of money we are working with."

160

"Agreed," I said simply as I stood up to follow her.

She knew exactly where to look for everything and was quickly picking up piles of mail and bills from the small desk in Charlie's room. She opened a drawer on the desk and pulled out a small key ring with one key on it and a piece of folded paper.

"What's that?" I asked her.

She held up the key and said, "This is for the safety deposit box." Then held up the paper and said, "This is the password list to his online accounts."

"Ahh," I nodded as I understood and she grabbed the stack of papers and key and went out to stack them on the dinette table near the kitchen.

Then she went into the guest room where I had been staying and she started rummaging through the desk with the computer monitor on it and handing me pieces of paper, bank statements and insurance records. When she was finished, she turned and took the papers from my hands and asked me to get the computer that was under the desk. I quickly scrambled to unplug everything from the box and picked it up. I didn't need the monitor or keyboard or any of the other things on the desk, I could set it up later with spare parts from other computers if I needed to.

Carrying the computer behind her, I followed Kelly back out into the apartment. She walked calmly over to the table behind the futon where Charlie's laptop was and picked it up. With both of our arms full, she turned back to look at me with a mix of grief, anxiousness and determination on her face.

"Let's go," she said as she gathered everything up in her arms with determination, "we're going to my place."

The aftermath…

I stayed with Kelly for a few weeks after Charlie's death. I wanted to be nearby to support her and to answer any questions that Charlie's mother, or the police, needed my help with. For the most part, I was concerned about Kelly. Just getting through the funeral, which she and I paid for, was tough enough on her.

I went with her to handle the most difficult things she had to deal with after that, like talking with Charlie's mom and going to Probate Court to establish her as the executor of Charlie's will. Kelly handled talking with the court better than with Charlie's mother. They both broke down in tears several times as the three of us met in Charlie's apartment. His mother was a little confused about why Kelly was the executor of his will but she listened to Kelly's explanation and nodded her head as Kelly told her what Charlie had said when he had the will drawn up.

Kelly offered his mother anything that she wanted from his apartment and the two of them spent a couple of hours going through his things. His mother took a few things from Charlie's younger years, like a picture album of their family, his high school diploma and a few items she had sent him as birthday and Christmas presents over the years. Both Kelly and I knew that Charlie was not that close to his mom but we knew that wasn't her fault; and we felt the sadness that was displayed on her face as she looked around his apartment.

After taking care of that, we didn't hear from his mother again. Kelly took little time in getting her own collection of Charlie's valuables that had meaning for her and held a series of 'garage sales' to empty his apartment of the rest of his belongings. It's funny, she called them 'garage sales' even though Charlie had no garage. Most of his things sold fairly quickly, the televisions and stereo items and other high-end things went quickly. When the apartment was down to just a small truckload of items left, she called a local charity and had them load the rest of it up as a donation. Then she worked with the apartment office to cancel the lease on Charlie's apartment. She cried through most of that, as it added a deeper and more final sense of closure to the life of our friend and her on-again, off-again boyfriend.

Once his physical belongings were taken care of, she worked on the paperwork to get the life insurance claim paid and the money in his bank accounts moved to hers. Charlie hadn't been exaggerating when he said that he still had quite a bit of his dad's money left over. We were both a little shocked at the balances in his accounts and how little debt he was carrying on his credit cards. We told each other several times that we'd rather have Charlie back than his money but in an unspoken way, the gifts he had given her would help us get our own lives in order.

It was about that time that we found out she was pregnant. We saw her doctor and, sure enough, she was with child. The doctor gave us enough information to know that it was my child and not Charlie's; but that wouldn't have mattered to either of us. We will raise the child as our own no matter what. Our main concern, actually, was that we needed to speed up our plans to get married to take care of the child properly. The news of the baby was actually the one small beacon of light and hope we'd had in some time since I started talking to Charlie about all of the crazy things he had been researching. It was a relief to both Kelly and me, a sort of physical 'sign' that our union together was blessed in some way…blessed with the promise of new life.

After Kelly had taken care of Charlie's things and her finances were in order, we made our plans to get married. We decided to go ahead and get married right away in her Methodist church, so we didn't have to wait until the baby was born first. Even though we had decided to convert to Catholicism later, we knew about their waiting periods and requirements; and rather than put Kelly and the child through the issues of 'single parenthood' we pushed forward with making the arrangements as soon as we could. Luckily Kelly had a pretty good relationship with her church's pastor and we were able to arrange for a very small ceremony in short notice. I confirmed with a local Catholic priest that the Church will allow for married couples of other denominations to convert as a couple, so we weren't worried about that part of it. We just needed to make it happen.

As for me, in the meantime while we waited for the wedding date to arrive, I went back home to get my things in order. I got a realtor and put my house on the market. I gave my pets to the woman who had watched them for me over the years when I travelled. She loved them and I couldn't see adding to Kelly and mine's worries about trying to move them with me, first to Tampa and then to wherever we ended up. I spent a few of weeks at the house separating everything I owned into two piles…the things I was going to move and the stuff I was going to sell. Along the way, I generated a third pile for things to donate to the local charities.

Like Kelly selling off Charlie's things, I held a series of weekend 'garage sales', and I actually had a garage, but I allowed many serious buyers to walk through the entire house to see if they wanted any of the larger furniture or high-end items I was getting rid of. It wasn't much work, after all I was nearly giving things away in my rush to get back to Florida and be with Kelly. Once the house was pretty much emptied out, I delivered what was left to the local charities and banked the money. I spent a few days in a hotel room while I worked with the realtor on the final details before heading back to Tampa. Our very small and quiet wedding was just days later.

Now married and her 'with child' we got busy getting ready to make our move. While I was away, she was holding garage sales of her own; trying to sell off the things she didn't need and make room for what little of my own stuff I brought with me. What I had was mostly stuff I needed for work, clothes and some personal items but nothing really that important. It was funny, really, in light of my conversations with Charlie and now married to Kelly with a baby on the way; a lot of things lost their importance with both of us. We had little trouble selling off our material possessions that no longer held any value as we prepared ourselves to move and for the arrival of our child.

We spent many hours at night talking about where we might move to. She and I both liked Florida well enough but we needed a place to start fresh, to get away from our old lives and start our new lives together somewhere. After some conversations and a few trips around the state, we decided on St. Augustine. The climate was similar, if not a bit cooler, than Tampa and being on the east coast it was far enough away to give us that sense of 'newness' we were looking for. We made a couple of trips and searched around for a place to live and schools and, most importantly, a church. We found several to choose from.

When we visited the Cathedral Basilica of Saint Augustine, we were filled with an overwhelming sense of 'home' and were equally amazed at the history and architecture. We spoke with a very friendly priest about our wanting to come into the Church and our imminent move to the area. He listened to our questions and answered them with a warm, fatherly manner. He gave us some materials on the parish and introduced us to the people who organized the adult program of conversion. They too were very friendly and welcoming to us and gave us some information to take with us about the program - The *Rite of Christian Initiation for Adults*, or RCIA as we would come to know it. They were very friendly and helpful and invited us to contact them as soon as we were settled in town.

After we left, we just happened to take a 'wrong turn' along the way back to the hotel and stumbled across a modest home that had a 'For Sale' sign in the yard. We stopped and looked around and found the place to be empty, with no apparent occupants. We saw that it had a fenced in back yard and was at least three bedrooms with a garage. There were some flyers in a plastic container attached to the sign in the yard, so we took one and looked it over. Sure enough, it was unoccupied and had four bedrooms which would work out better for us having a baby on the way and my needing a room for an office for my work. It was priced within our range and, as we scanned the exterior and looked in through the windows, appeared to be in pretty good shape.

As we drove away, Kelly and I talked about how much of a coincidence it was that we ran across the place. We both grinned and winked at each other, sharing our own silent joke about 'coincidences' of this sort. We had the information to contact the realtor, so I called him to find out if we could see the inside of the house. He told us he was on his way over to it even as we spoke, which I repeated so Kelly could hear, and told me he could show us the house in a few minutes. Upon hearing the conversation and before I could hang up, Kelly stopped her car and turned it around. She drove us back to the house and we sat in the driveway waiting for the realtor to arrive.

He showed up just a few minutes later, commenting on 'what a coincidence' it was that we called when we did. We both nodded in agreement and I couldn't help but let out a chuckle at his remark. Kelly giggled too but when he asked what we were laughing about, we waved him off and started asking about the house. He got quickly down to business and unlocked the front door to let us in. He gave us the tour, pointed out some of the highlights and answered our questions. The place really was in great shape and we really liked the kitchen. The realtor told us that the owner was eager to sell the house and admitted that he was on his way over to put a 'Price Reduced' sign on the 'For Sale' sign out front.

Kelly and I looked at each other and smiled. I leaned over and whispered to her, "What do you think?"

She whispered back, "I think it's perfect" and kissed me on the cheek.

We turned and I told the realtor not to put the 'Price Reduced' sign out front and instead to put a 'Sold' sign out. He looked at us nearly in shock, as I'm sure he didn't expect to have a sale go so quickly. What he didn't realize what how much Kelly and I wanted to get moved to St. Augustine and that we had quite a bit of money in the bank to help us out.

That afternoon we spent a couple of hours at the realtor's office signing papers and putting our bid on the house. As if to seal the deal, my cell phone rang as he was calling the owners to let them know of our offer. I answered the phone and found out from my realtor back home that my house had an offer made on it. Without hesitation I told her to tell the buyers I would take their offer and to send me the papers I needed to sign right away. My heart was relieved and lifted to have that taken care of and knew in my heart that these things were all falling in to place to help Kelly and me get moved, get settled and get into the Church.

As we lay in the hotel room bed later that night, I softly caressed her stomach marveling at how our luck had turned for the good on this trip. I asked her about selling her beauty shop and her own home and what she thought of our plan so far.

"I am really starting to believe that we are doing exactly what we need to be doing right now, for the first time in my life I really believe that," she confided to me. "As soon as we get back we'll list my house with a realtor and, as for my business, there's a woman I know who has been offering to buy it from me for years. She's one of my competitors and has been after my client base for some time now. I'll call her as soon as we're back in Tampa."

Once we got back to her place, we both became very serious and committed to moving across the state. Kelly called the woman she had mentioned about her business and had an offer in a few hours. They talked back and forth a few times making offers and counter-offers until finally Kelly heard a number she felt good about. I heard her voice from the next room saying, "Just send me the paperwork as soon as you can."

She came in to the dining room where I was sitting with my laptop looking for potential work and announced that her salon would be sold by the end of the week. I stood and hugged her tightly and could feel her heart pounding as fast as my own, the excitement of our move building with each step. Later that day, she called her own realtor and started the work to put her house up for sale.

Things were moving so quickly at that point. The next day, the paperwork to sell my house came in the mail and I quickly scanned, copied and signed the documents and put them in an overnight delivery envelope to send them back. Since the house was empty, the buyers had chosen a closing date that was just a week away and that was fine with me as I was eager to sell the place and get the money in the bank. I had given my realtor power of attorney to conduct the closing without me, so with the papers I had just signed in her hands, she would be able to close the deal without my having to be there. Again, my heart felt lifted at the relief of yet another 'To Do' crossed off of my mental list.

Sure enough, Kelly had a check in her hand as she came home that Friday and told me that the new owner had the keys, deed and everything else she'd need to take over the salon. She was so full of excitement she literally bubbled with joy as we hugged and kissed in celebration. Later that same day, my realtor called to let me know that the money from the sale of my house would be mailed out to me the next week. Again, when I told Kelly about it we both were filled with excitement and relief. On the following Monday, the realtor from St. Augustine called us to let us know the owner of that house had accepted our offer and wanted to know when we'd like to close. We told him as soon as possible and he said he would try to get us in the house as soon as he could.

In the meantime, Kelly and I literally ran around her house packing our things up in boxes. Over the next couple of weeks, her house looked more and more like a storage facility as the boxes started piling up. We frantically raced around the place getting ourselves ready to move. Soon, we were down to just the large furniture and enough of the kitchen items that we could still cook as we waited for news on the loan and the house in St. Augustine. That didn't take much time, all things considered, mainly because we both had pretty good credit and with the two of us together, we actually had enough money in the bank to buy it without a loan; but we wanted to hold on to as much money as we could to live on, so we still applied for a mortgage on the house.

We were packed and ready and waiting to go, our nerves were on edge as we tried to be as patient as we could. Finally, a week later, we got the call that everything was settled and we made a date to close on the house and take immediate occupancy a week later. We were overjoyed and filled with hope and optimism, which was really a surprise considering how dark and foreboding our lives had been leading up to Charlie's death. In fact, the frantic pace that we were keeping in getting everything sold off and ready to move helped to keep our minds off of dwelling on all of the sadness and grief that had only been a few months earlier. I remember pondering on how things like that just seem to work out sometimes. More coincidences.

Soon enough, the time flew by and we were on our way to St. Augustine in Kelly's Mustang. All of our belongings and my car were being taken there by the movers and were a few days ahead of us. We were all smiles as we drove with the wind blowing in through the slightly opened windows; and we chatted like teenagers at all the things we were going to do once we got there. We did get there, closed on the house the next day and had the keys to the house in hand that afternoon. One last night in a hotel room and we'd be in our new home. We were very excited and talked about more about the house and all of the things we needed to do and were looking forward to with this new chapter of our lives.

As we lay in bed in the hotel room that night, we made love in a way that was a celebration of new life, our new home and our new town. In the aftermath of being together, we finally calmed down after weeks of excitement in getting ourselves moved and I remembered the seriousness of why we were doing all of this. I reminded Kelly that we needed to remember the reasons we were moving and starting our lives over in this new town. Her face grew serious as I talked to her, reminding her of our promise to join the Church and how much we needed to go through with all of it.

She agreed and we laid there side-by-side in silence for awhile, each of us lost in our own thoughts. I saw a tear roll slowly down her cheek and knew she was remembering Charlie and his tragic accident. I thought about him myself and my promises to him. So far we had kept to the plan but there was still some work to do. We still needed to join the Church, we still needed to find a boat, and I needed to get busy writing down all he had told me. Kelly interrupted my thoughts by rolling over and holding me tightly. I caressed her arm and kissed her and we fell asleep holding each other.

The next day, it was back to a frantic pace as we got to the house and met the movers. We were surprised at how quickly they unpacked the boxes from their truck and tried to keep up with them as we directed them to this room and that to get the boxes and furniture located where we wanted the stuff placed. A few hours later and Kelly and I stood alone amidst piles of boxes in our new home. Then it was all up to us to unpack and get settled in. The first few days we focused on the things we needed to live...the kitchen ware and the bathroom items that we'd need to function day-to-day. After that, we took our time unloading the boxes and decorating the house.

While Kelly was now focused on the décor, I worked on getting my office functional. Frantically, I set up the computers and printers and other things I needed to do my consulting work and write down Charlie's story. The time seemed to fly by with all of the activity going on and before we knew it, it was the end of the week and we needed to get ready for the weekend. I called the RCIA coordinators and confirmed that we were in town and we were really looking forward to starting the classes so we could join the Church come Easter time. I was relieved yet again at how enthusiastic they were and seemed to be eager to meet us again.

That first Sunday, we attended the class and we were really surprised at how much of what they were telling us made sense, particularly in light of how little we actually knew about the Church. Like most Protestants coming in, we had our own ideas of what we thought the Church believed, having been told so by the media and the people we talked with over the years. We were surprised at how wrong we were about many of the things we thought the Catholics taught; and we eagerly participated by asking questions and reading the notes they handed out.

We were invited to stay after the class that day by the priest who had given the class. He was one of three priests in the parish and, as we answered his questions, he became more and more curious about us and our story. We shared a little of it with him. I didn't tell him or Kelly all the things Charlie and I had discussed; but enough to let him know we knew a little more than some others about the Bible. He offered to be our spiritual director that day and gave us his card, telling us to call or email him if we had questions outside of class. We were both grateful for his interest in us and I was personally very relieved to have someone of his knowledge level to be able to ask the more difficult questions that I would not, or could not, ask in class…for fear of scaring the other class members.

We were invited to Mass later that day and we went; and even though we weren't in the Church yet we both felt moved by it. Even Kelly commented on how the Mass was like a scene right out of the Bible on our way home. I agreed with her but didn't tell her that it pretty much was, exactly that, a scene right out of Revelations no less. I didn't tell Kelly a lot of the thoughts I had, thanks to my talks with Charlie, as I didn't want to scare her too much. It was all so confusing at that point, the incredible downward spiral that Charlie's conversations had taken me right up to his death; and then the amazing sense of being uplifted through our marriage, Kelly's pregnancy and our move to St. Augustine and now our journey into the Church.

It wasn't all easy, though. It was a bit of a struggle at first getting used to the idea of living life the right way. We got rid of all of Charlie's pornography and drug related things when we had packed up our belongings at Kelly's house before the move. Even though we knew what we were doing was right and that those things were bad, we still were overcome by memories of him and our time together as we sorted through his stuff and threw it in the trash. We both agreed to stay away from any drugs that were not legal ever again; and Kelly even told me she wasn't going to drink alcohol either, at least not while she was pregnant. I was moved by her sacrifice and loved her even more as I could see she was starting to care more about the baby than herself. I couldn't make that same promise, however, because I knew I had to write Charlie's story and, to be honest, I'd probably need a drink or two to keep the nightmares out of my dreams.

We had promised the RCIA coordinators that we'd do all of the readings to catch up to the classes, and we both did. Having Kelly and I going through the notes together was a true blessing, as we could talk with each other about them and discuss them prior to going to the classes. For her, it was like a journey up a mountain. For me, the process was more like a roller coaster. At night, after she went to bed, I started writing Charlie's story. Reading the RCIA materials and going to the classes was uplifting; and at nights while writing down all of Charlie's interpretations it felt like falling again. Up and down, hope and destruction, theology and prophecy…my journey was much more tumultuous than Kelly's. I was worried that we were both spending too much time out of work and we'd go through the money we had too quickly. Still, it was sort of a blessing that we had the time off together, to go through what we were learning about the Church together and work on it as a couple. I kept reminding myself of that as the time passed.

I tried to keep the conflicting feelings from her but she was too observant. She asked me one day what was wrong and I lied and said, "Nothing." Of course, she knew better and pressed me and I confided to her that I was writing about Charlie and trying to connect the things he had told me with what the Church notes were teaching and that sometimes, it was very difficult. She recommended that I email the priest from RCIA class and ask him if I had a tough question. I told her I would and then changed the subject quickly to something about the house or asking if she was having any luck finding work. That was usually enough to get her mind off of what was on my mind and we'd talk about something else for awhile.

The weeks went by and slowly the house started looking more like a home. I was making good progress with Charlie's story during the late nights and, at the same time, learning a tremendous amount of information on the Church and her teachings. I much liked the 'motherly' aspect of the Church and her view of the Virgin Mary; and was reminded of that every time I looked at Kelly and her growing belly. I thought too about the 'fatherly' nature of God and how the Church teaches that as the Trinity, God is actually a Divine Family. Those kinds of thoughts made me smile, especially when Kelly was around and I could see our own family growing inside her.

At other times, though, in the middle of the night while going through Charlie's notes and remembering our conversations, hope seemed to fade a bit as I typed his thoughts on Armageddon and the end of the world and all of the horrors that were to come; and fairly soon according to his theories. Watching the evening news and keeping up with world events on the Internet weren't helping either. The wars going on in the Middle East and the growing problems with the global economy kept peeling away the layers of hope and optimism that the Church and Kelly brought me during the daytime. The morning we got the call that someone put a bid on her house in Tampa was a tremendous relief for the both of us, since it was the last tie to the 'old lives' we had left behind and it was going to put a little more money in the bank for us to live on until we got our careers back in order. Then again, that same night while I was working on Charlie's book I saw that the stock market had dipped in response to some nasty fighting going on in the Middle East and it took me back down a notch.

Still, thanks to the classes and talking with the priest and listening at Mass; there were some messages that got through to me. Like, for one thing, we are all going to die someday and most of us have no idea when or how but if we have faith and live according to God's law, we shouldn't worry about it too much. Death was our entry way into Heaven, so in a strange way, I started to look at death differently. It was no longer such a bad prospect, considering we had Heaven as our destination. I kept reminding myself of that night after night as I wrote Charlie's story down in the darkness of my office at the other end of the hall where Kelly slept.

Looking back, it was kind of strange how I'd work on a particular part of Charlie's story and remember his ideas on what this or that meant and then in RCIA class, I'd hear what the Church teaches about those same things. There were some concepts that Charlie was quite correct with, like the Catholic Church being the 'one true church' and how the various schisms had fractured out over the course of history. One difference on that topic was finding out just how compassionate and tolerant the Church was with the Protestants and even the Muslims. I mean, of course they don't teach that the others are 'right' but they do respect that we all worship the same God, even if not completely correctly. Charlie's opinions of them were much more derisive.

Different, also, are the reasons for it. The Catholics aren't the 'one true church' because they invented Christianity; rather it was given to them by God himself. They didn't just make it up, they are passing it along; and they are the only Church with a clear, unbroken line of authority all the way back to the original Apostles who were given the traditions, teachings and keys of authority from Christ himself. All of that is right there in the Gospels. Everything we are learning about is deeply rooted in the Bible, actually, from the authority of the Pope to the Eucharist and all of the sacraments and traditions. A lot of modern Protestants like to claim that the Church isn't 'Biblical' but the irony is, the Bible was born out of the Church, not the other way around.

Besides that, modern Protestants don't even follow what the founders of their denominations actually believed. Luther, Calvin and the others all believed in things like honoring Mary, the 'real presence' in the Eucharist and a bunch of other Church teachings that their modern followers argue about with the Church. In fact, most all Protestants I know of nowadays can explain all of the reasons why they aren't Catholic or what about the Church they don't believe; but oddly enough, most of them can't tell you why they are in the denomination they are in. Most might say it's how they were brought up but if you were to ask a Baptist why they aren't a Lutheran; or why a Methodist isn't a Presbyterian...they can't answer the question because they really don't even know what the differences are or the histories of their own church, for that matter. But I digress.

Another interesting topic in RCIA class was the woman in the Revelations story, who the Church teaches is a figure of both the Church itself and the Virgin Mary after being crowned Queen of Heaven and Earth. Charlie's view was that she somehow represented the world and the 'baby' she bore early on was the New World of the America's. I suppose they both could be right, in some way, but I forego asking any in-depth questions whenever that particular book comes up in classes or at Mass. Actually, although I am learning more and more about how the Church interprets that book of the Bible, I cannot help but cringe in fear every time its name is even mentioned. One particular class that was very difficult for me was the one on 'the four last things'; namely: Death, Judgment, Heaven and Hell. I could barely choke down the coffee and donuts they provided when that particular lesson was taught, as the memories of my conversations with Charlie sprang to mind.

Still further, Charlie was right about the end of this world...it will happen and I am certain that it will happen in a way that fulfills the prophecies in some way. The Church also teaches this but she teaches something else more important: that we shouldn't dwell on how or when the specific events take place but that for each of us individually; we should always be ready. For each of us, our own deaths mark the 'end of the world' from our perspective and whether we die alone in a hospital bed or as a result of a massive earthquake, we should be prepared. There are, after all, only two choices after this world – life or death, Heaven or Hell; and we should be using our time here to get ready for our 'just rewards'. Luckily, Kelly and I are choosing life...eternal life. We still have a few things to finish first, though. We still have to get confirmed in the Church, we need to eat the Bread of Life, and we still have to have our first confessions. We've been preparing ourselves for it and will soon pour out our sinful lives on the ears of one of the priests and pray for God's mercy. In going through the memories of our past lives, I'll just say that our lists are a bit longer than we'd originally thought they'd be.

One of the nicer things I have learned, I should mention, is that there are two stories going on in Revelations and most people, Charlie included, tend to be preoccupied with the 'horror story' part of it that details the end of the world and the coming Day of Judgment. It's the other part of the story that captures my attention now, especially in Mass, in that woven in to all of the talk of death and destruction is a beautiful image of the eternal worship in Heaven. It is a story of altars and angels, incense and prayers, psalms and hymns, redemption and deliverance; which is missed by most people but is actually describing the how similar the Masses on earth mirror the eternal Mass in Heaven. In fact, every time a Mass is conducted in the world Heaven and Earth actually meet, they are connected in the one thing that matters – glorifying God.

Kelly and I have made drastic changes in our lives. We now pray every day. We learned how to pray the rosary and we pray it every night together. We pray for ourselves and our baby. We pray for our family and friends. We pray for our nation and the whole world, and for the conversion of Russia. Most importantly, we pray for our poor friend Charlie and hope against hope that God will have mercy on him. We know that even with all of his faults, even with all of the sinful things he was doing before he died; the one thing he did have going for him was his search for the Truth. Even though he may have been looking for it in the wrong places, or looking for it in the wrong ways, he was doubtful enough in the end that we pray he lived just long enough after being hit by that truck to ask God for forgiveness and mercy.

All in all, it's been a crazy experience. Since I first decided to make the trip to Tampa to see my old high school friends, to moving to St. Augustine married to Kelly with a child on the way and joining the Church; I could not have foreseen any of it. Now that I have Charlie's story written down, the dark nights alone in my office with all of his theories and interpretations are behind me. The book is written and I'm happy to be done with it. I now have more time to spend with Kelly and focus on our family yet to be born. I still have to find a boat and learn how to drive it but, in the meantime, Kelly is making plans to start another beauty salon after the baby is born and I am trying to find some new work. We are both busy getting our lives ready to come into the Church on Easter; and becoming parents in the summer.

The End.

www.ingramcontent.com/pod-product-compliance
Lightning Source LLC
Chambersburg PA
CBHW030331020726
47493CB00004B/1238